Melee

Melee

Kristy Tate

Indie Artist Press / Brackettville, Texas

Melee
A novel by Kristy Tate
First Paperback Edition
Copyright © Kristy Tate 2019
All Rights Reserved
Printed in the United States of America
ISBN-13:978-1-62522-131-5

Publisher Information-
Indie Artist Press
P. O. Box 131
Brackettville, TX 78832
www.indieartistpress.com

One

As sunlight touched the eastern sky Declan sat up, shivering. Brushing twigs and leaves off his naked skin, he crawled to huddle behind a huckleberry bush to make sense of things. His whole world tilted as he tried to process what had happened. He had spent the night in the woods. Naked? How could he have forgotten something as important as his clothes?

Beyond the woods, Lizbet's house. Only the barn stirred with life. Horses nickered, goats bleated, pigs snorted—all were waiting for their breakfast, and Declan knew who would provide it. Lizbet. He couldn't face her. Not like this. After shooting a quick glance at the house, wondering if anyone was awake to witness his streaking, he ran for his car.

The keys. Where were they? In the pocket of his jeans. But where were his pants? Crouching behind the Mercedes, he spotted them—or what was left of them—at the edge of the woods. He commando crawled through the tall grass, snake-like, flinching as twigs and pebbles poked and pierced his skin. All his clothes had been ripped to shreds, but thankfully, his keys were still in the remains of his pocket. He scooped up the cottony threads of what had once been his clothes.

His shivering accelerated as he pressed the key fob, crawled back through the grass, avoiding anything sharp or dangerous looking, and lifted the car's door handle. Inside the Mercedes, he started the engine and turned up the heater full blast. He glanced in the rearview mirror, half-expecting to see a furry snout instead of his nose and unshaved chin. He looked exactly like himself, but... he gazed at his arms and chest... different. He studied the wolf bite on his hand. A few hours ago the puncture wounds had been a bloody mess, but it had since healed to a pink line. Strange.

By the time he arrived at his grandfather's house in the University District, he had practically convinced himself that it had all been a bad dream.

But his shredded clothes told a different story.

He collapsed onto his bed just after dawn and fell into a restless sleep.

Lizbet addressed a crowd of gathered animals. "I really appreciate your willingness to put aside your animosity to fight our common enemy. As you know, a pack of wolves has been terrorizing our community. There have even been some deaths."

Chattering, growling, and murmuring rippled through the crowd.

"It needs to stop," Lizbet said. "And I believe it can. But only if we all work together."

A crow fluttered to perch on Lizbet's shoulder. It whispered in her ear and she stopped and slowly turned in Declan's direction. He thought about hiding, but realized he could never do so from the birds.

"What are you doing here, Declan?" she asked, her voice hard.

He stepped out from behind the tree, amazed to find he was almost as scared of Lizbet as he was of the bear. "What—" His voice cracked. He cleared his throat and tried again. "What are you doing?"

She twisted her lips together and scowled at him. He could tell she was battling between the truth and a lie. Finally, she said, "I'm going to catch a werewolf."

Drenched in sweat, Declan bolted up, kicking the covers off his bed. He swung his legs off the side of the bed and sat with his elbows on his knees and his head in his hands. He willed his heart to stop racing. It's only a dream, he told himself. But it was more than that. It was a memory. A painful one.

And if it was a memory, it meant that the other, more terrifying dreams could also be memories. He padded over to his computer, sat down in front of it, and turned it on.

He typed "night terrors" into the search engine.

> *Episodes usually occur 1 to 2 hours after going to sleep and can last from 1 to 30 minutes. The victim will look like himself with open eyes but his expression will be vacant, if not horror-struck. Waking a victim will prove difficult, if not impossible. Upon waking, he or she won't remember the incident, no matter what terror he has endured.*
>
> *During an episode, it is typical for one to exhibit intense fear or agitation. They may be violent. They will not be cognizant of their surroundings. Their breathing may quicken and their heartrate increase. They may perspire profusely. They may scream and try to fight demons that only they can see.*
>
> *Night terrors are different from nightmares. Nightmares are frightening dreams that can often be recalled the next morning in vivid detail. Night terrors leave no trace in the memory.*

That was it. Night terrors. Although, according to this article, victims of night terrors were usually under the age of twelve. But Declan wrote off his experience in the woods as night terrors—a phenomenon brought on by the shock of Lizbet's revelations. For that, of course, he couldn't manufacture a rational explanation without engaging in a losing argument with her—and maybe a bear or a skunk. No sense in picking a fight he had no chance of winning.

But as for his own personal nightmare—he didn't need to revisit it.

He hoped.

It was only a little after six. He could sleep for another couple of hours. But *could* and *would* were two very different concepts. Silently, he crept from his room and down the hall and peeked through his mom's ajar bedroom door. She slept curled in a ball in the middle of her king-size bed, the bedclothes wrapped around her legs, her arms tucked under her. He tiptoed across the long stretch of carpet, passing through a swath of early morning light streaming through the window. In her bathroom, he found her collection of medicine in the cabinet. He grabbed four bottles, and after another glance at his mom, he took them into her closet and closed the door before flipping on the light.

The sudden brightness stung his eyes. It took a moment for his vision to clear. Surrounded by his mom's power suits, silky dresses, and shoes, he scanned the medicine labels before selecting the one that read, *For relief of sleeplessness when associated with pain.*

He knew what he was doing was wrong, but he rationalized away his guilt. He told himself emotional pain was just as real as physical pain. He swallowed the pills dry.

Elizabeth stood in the far corner of her garden waving

her cane at a flock of sparrows.

"Something wrong, Grandma?" Lizbet asked, coming up behind her.

"These dad-gum birds are eating all of my grapes!" Elizabeth groused.

"They have to feed their families, too," Lizbet said gently as she eyed the small, hard green balls that had weeks to go before being palatable to anyone other than the sparrows.

Elizabeth blew out a sigh. "You sound like you're on their side!"

"I didn't know there were any sides," Lizbet said. "I'm just pointing out—"

"Ugh. You sound like Josie!" Elizabeth sloshed through the muddy garden patch. "She's always trying to get me to sell this place."

That was not only unfair, but it was also untrue. "I don't want you to sell the ranch, and I know my mom doesn't either."

Elizabeth sniffed as she moved between the corn stalks. Some had already grown past her shoulders while others barely reached her waist. A few of the taller stalks had baby ears of corn and sported puffs of silk.

"This place is my life," Elizabeth said. "I wouldn't know what to do with myself if I had to vegetate in Josie's condo all day."

Lizbet trailed after her grandmother. Because she was a good five inches shorter than her grandmother, some of the stalks touched her hair and threatened to poke her in the eye with their floppy leaves. "No one is asking you to move in with Josie."

Elizabeth made a harrumphing sound. "We're going to have to make some salsa out of these tomatoes," she said. "If we can keep the deer out of here."

Lizbet took note of the hundreds of nearly ripe tomatoes. Only a few, that she could see, had deer bites in them. "I think the critters have shown a lot of self-restraint," Lizbet said.

Elizabeth turned and gave her an are-you-insane look.

"Come on, Grandma," Lizbet said, taking Elizabeth's arm. "Let's go and make some lunch."

When an invitation to Nicole's going away party coincided with the first night of August's full moon, only a niggle of warning flashed in the back of Declan's mind.

"Are you sure you want to go?" Declan asked Lizbet as they browsed the bookstore for used textbooks. He would be a freshman at the University of Washington at the end of September and Lizbet would start classes at Queen Anne Community College a couple of weeks before that.

"Sure, why not?" Lizbet flipped her curls over her shoulder and gave him a smile that sent him over the moon.

"Well, it's not as if you're friends..."

"But she's your friend, right?"

"Yeah, but..."

"Come on, it'll be good for me. I'm trying to be more social." She bumped him with her hip before moving down the aisle. She glanced at her list of required books for the upcoming semester.

"You're plenty social." Declan trailed after her, but stopped as a title caught his eye.

The Meaning and Translation of Dreams. He pulled it off the shelf and flipped it open.

People who are anxious or overtired are more likely to sleepwalk or experience sleep terrors. A relaxing routine paired with an early bedtime can help prevent sleep disturbances.

Avoid sleepwalking injuries by making the bedroom and house as safe as possible. Consider the following precautions:

Make sure there are no sharp or breakable objects near the bed.

Install gates on stairways.

Lock doors and windows.

If psychological stress contributes to disordered sleep, counseling may help. Both children and adults may benefit from hypnosis or biofeedback.

In some cases, a doctor may prescribe short-acting sleep or antianxiety medications to reduce or eliminate episodes.

Seek professional help if:

• Episodes are frequent or severe.

• The sleepwalker gets injured during episodes.

• The sleepwalker leaves the house.

• Nighttime episodes are accompanied by daytime sleepiness.

Stress, anxiety or other psychological factors may be contributing to sleep disturbances.

Sleepwalkers occasionally injure themselves or others. But most episodes of sleepwalking and sleep terrors are brief and harmless.

Lizbet glanced over his shoulder. "What's this?"

He slammed the book shut. "Nothing."

"You having problems sleeping?"

"Not really. Just that one night." He slipped the book back onto the shelf.

"What night?" she pressed.

He shrugged her question off. "Listen. It makes sense. Talking animals, werewolves, and were-Schnauzers. Anyone would have nightmares. It was a lot to process." A sudden memory assaulted him and he closed his eyes, trying to tune it out.

Hunger burned the back of his throat and tightened his gut. He padded across the forest floor. A carpeting of pine needles and soft soil muffled his footfalls. Above the trees' canopy, a smattering of stars glistened, pale against a cloud-filled night. Mist shrouded the round, full strawberry moon.

He sat back on his haunches and lifted his head toward the moon. Snatches of conversations drifted by. Apprehension surged through his blood. He gazed at his paw...so foreign. How had he transformed into this creature? On all fours, he loped through the woods aimlessly, fighting the hunger that zinged through his veins.

"Of course." Lizbet looped her arm around his and pulled him into a sideways hug and out of the memory. Hallucination. Nightmare...whatever it was.

"It's amazing that we're both not bonkers," she said.

"Bonkers," he murmured. His gaze landed on another book, *Mental Health for Dummies.*

He needed help.

Music thrummed through the open windows. Someone had hung a disco ball from the dining room chandelier and shafts of multicolored light sparkled on the dark lawn. Kids in jeans, T-shirts, and UW hoodies lounged on the front porch. Lizbet wanted to belong, but she still felt like a poser. This was Declan's world, as foreign to her as the moon.

She picked out Baxter, Declan's oversized friend, Maria, her neighbor, and McNally, another teammate of Declan's from East End High's basketball team all standing in a tight circle just inside the double-wide doors. She tightened her grip on Declan's hand.

He wore jeans, flip-flops, and a Twenty One Pilots T-shirt. Trying to fit in, she'd chosen a nearly identical outfit, but her T-shirt and jeans couldn't hide her curves...and nothing could tame her curls.

As if sensing her insecurity, Declan dropped a quick kiss on her temple.

"Who's that with Nicole?" she asked, nodding at a guy with a Cross-Fitter's build leaning against the porch railing, his eyes trained on Nicole, a lithe blonde with flushed cheeks.

"Jason Norbit. Her old squeeze. They broke up a while ago."

"You mean when she applied to Duke?"

Declan dipped his chin. "He's going to UW on a football scholarship."

Lizbet bit her bottom lip as she followed Declan up the porch steps and through the doorway. She had her own theories about why Nicole had applied to Duke.

Nicole was beautiful in an ice-queen way. Her home had the same understated elegance—the disco ball being the notable exception. Someone had carried the dining room table out through the French doors to the back patio and people danced on the hardwood floor beneath the spinning lights.

"Want to dance?" Declan asked.

"No." The thought horrified her. She'd never danced in front of a crowd before. Her thoughts flitted back to

the first time she had ever danced...with Declan...in the moonlight. Dancing had turned to kissing. That had been a first for her, too. "Do you?"

He shook his head, grinned as if he shared her memories, and put his hand on her shoulder to steer her outside to his cluster of friends surrounding the food-piled dining room table.

Nicole waylaid them. "Hey, Declan. Any second thoughts about ditching Duke?"

Declan shook his head. "Sorry, Nicki, you're on your own."

Jason pulled himself away from the wall and draped his arm across Nicole's shoulder. "Not quite on her own. There's only about three thousand in the freshman class."

Lizbet wasn't sure, but she thought she saw a flicker of irritation in Nicole's eyes.

McNally appeared at Declan's side and elbowed him. "Yeah, now that you're going to UW, have you thought about playing intermural basketball?"

"Basketball?" A girl Lizbet didn't know broke into the conversation. "That's no fun. What about ultimate frisbee?" She flashed Declan a smile full of perfectly straight, bright white teeth. "That's co-ed."

"How about you?" Jason nodded at Lizbet. "Where you headed?"

"Queen Anne Community," Lizbet said. "Staying local."

Jason's gaze swept over her and lingered on her lips.

"Me, too." He lifted his soda bottle as if to clink her invisible goblet in a toast.

Lizbet sent Declan a quick glance, but he was lost in conversation with McNally and the unknown girl, debating the virtues of basketball and ultimate frisbee.

Jason leaned forward, placing his hand on the wall directly behind Lizbet and making her feel pinned. "What's your story?"

Lizbet knew he wouldn't believe her if she were stupid enough to tell him. She tested him. "Well, last month I killed a werewolf. How about you?"

He laughed as if she were joking. "So you're like Buffy? A vampire slayer?"

"No vampires," she said in all seriousness. "I tend to stick to creatures."

He nodded and a glint she didn't like filled his eyes.

"Seriously," she said. "I'm auditing a mythology class from Professor Madison at the University of Washington right now."

"What are you going to do with that? Kill more werewolves?"

"I'd rather just scare them away."

He snorted. "You're a tiny thing. It's hard to believe you could scare anything."

She blinked at him. "You'd be surprised."

"You're like a werewolf warrior?"

She wanted to smile to show him his invasion of her

personal space wasn't making her crazy, but the closer Jason pressed, the more uncomfortable she felt. She looked over his shoulder for Declan, but couldn't see him. Everyone else had deserted the porch and gone inside. Annoyance flashed through her. She spotted a cat sitting on the windowsill, watching them with slit eyes. She crooked a finger at the animal. He responded by twitching his whiskers.

Jason flicked a glance over his shoulder before turning back to Lizbet. The cat stood, arched his back, and batted a dead moth out of the corner of the window toward Jason's crotch. Surprised, Jason jumped out of the line of fire.

Lizbet's lips twitched as she escaped. "Thanks," she whispered to the cat as she went to find Declan. She didn't see him with his friends in the backyard, in the mass of kids huddled in the kitchen, or in any of the circles of conversation in the living room. She thought she heard his laughter floating up the stairwell that led to the basement, but before she climbed halfway down, someone turned off the lights and plunged the basement into inky darkness.

"Everyone close your eyes," a girl said.

Lizbet froze on the stairs, unsure where to go or what to do. She risked tripping in the dark in either direction.

"Vampire, open your eyes and select your victim." Someone switched on a flashlight and a girl giggled.

Lizbet hurried down the stairs.

"Stop! Intruder!" Someone turned on the overhead

light amidst groans.

Lizbet swallowed hard, suddenly aware that somehow she'd inadvertently pooped on the party.

The girl who seemed to be in charge pointed at Lizbet. "State your name and business." She had a severe haircut and wore I-mean-business glasses, a black turtleneck despite the warm summer night, and a pair of painted-on jeans.

"She's Lizbet and she's with me." Jason came up behind her and placed a heavy hand on her shoulder. "'Scuse us for interrupting. Mind if we join you?"

A couple of people made groaning sounds, but most murmured a welcome. The lights were doused before Lizbet even got a look around the room to see if Declan was in the crowd.

Jason tugged at her hand and she fell into a cross-legged position beside him. "I don't know this game," she whispered as she disentangled her fingers.

"It's easy. You'll catch on." Jason's warm breath fanned against her cheek. "As a werewolf warrior, you'll be a natural."

In the darkness, he seemed closer than she would have guessed. She inched away from him and bumped someone next to her. "Sorry," she hissed and held herself very still so as not to touch anyone else.

"Night has fallen...again," the game-master girl began. "While the villagers sleep, the vampire works the wages of death. Vampire, open your eyes and select your victim."

"Keep your eyes closed," Jason whispered, and he squeezed Lizbet's knee.

Moments later, the game-master girl flipped on a flashlight. "Everyone open your eyes." She flicked the flashlight at the faces of the twenty or so kids seated on the basement rug. When Lizbet saw Declan wasn't in their number, she wanted to leave, but she'd already interrupted the game once and didn't want to do it again.

"In the dark of night, a vampire stole into the home at twenty-eight Reynolds."

"Yeah! That's my house!" a redheaded kid with a smattering of freckles said.

The game-master girl slid him the evil eye. "While Carl slept, the vampire sucked his blood and left his lifeless body on the library floor."

"I have a library. Cool," Carl said.

"Yeah, like that's going to do you any good seeing as how you don't read," someone said.

"Hush!" a girl in a vintage Van Halen T-shirt hissed.

"You can't talk," a guy with hair like a hedgehog said. "You're dead."

Carl looked as if he wanted to argue, but he bit his tongue.

"I'm not sure I want to play this game," Lizbet whispered to Jason.

"You better be quiet, or else the vampire will kill you, too," Jason whispered.

"I'd be okay with that," Lizbet returned, "seeing as how

I don't want to play."

"Silence!" the game-master girl called out. "Villagers, who among you executed this dastardly deed?" she asked as she flashed the light into the blinking faces of her friends. "Who is the vampire?"

Speculations and laughter flew. Lizbet tried to be a good sport, but with Jason's thigh pressing against hers, she felt increasingly uncomfortable. The guy sitting on her other side had excessive arm and leg hair so that every time she bumped into him she felt like she was touching a fur ball. Plus, he had onion breath.

"Okay! New round!" The game-master girl stood and flipped on the overhead light, illuminating the orange shag carpet and plaid sofas pushed up against the wood-paneled walls. "Everyone turn in your cards."

Lizbet had missed something.

Declan, Baxter, and McNally followed by Nicole and a couple of girls trooped down the stairs.

"Hey, can we join in?" Baxter asked. Lizbet had observed that because Baxter was so big, people rarely told him no. The circle widened to let him in while Declan inserted himself next to Lizbet.

"What brought you down here?" Declan whispered in her ear.

"I was looking for you."

"Hmm, I was looking for you, too." He kissed her lightly on the lips.

"Not yet, Lamb."

"Sorry," Declan said, sounding not in the least repentant.

Nicole, who had wedged herself on the other side of Jason, rolled her eyes.

The game-master girl hit the lights. "Villagers, close your eyes! Night has fallen in the village of the doomed. While the villagers slumber, the vampire stalks his prey."

Someone dropped in front of Lizbet and planted a sloppy wet kiss on her lips. She struggled and pushed him off.

"Yeah! That's the game!" Jason said.

"Sorry, I..." Lizbet jumped to her feet. "I told you I didn't want to play." Embarrassed, she crawled over people in the dark until she found the stairs and felt her way out of the basement. In the kitchen, she realized that Declan had followed her.

"Ugh." She covered her face with her hands. "That was awful."

He laughed. "Don't let Jason hear you say that."

She shuddered. "Can we go?"

"Sure." He draped his arm around her shoulder. "It was just a game."

"I know. It wasn't a big deal." But it felt like it was.

Chapter 2

The next day, while Maria helped Lizbet pick the green beans from Lizbet's mom's garden, Maria told Lizbet that she wasn't the only one who had thought Jason kissing her was more of a big deal.

"Nicole was really mad," Maria told her.

"Why? I thought they broke up months ago."

Maria dropped a handful of beans into a basket. "They were getting back together." She lowered her voice to a whisper. "Her parents don't know it yet, but Nicole is thinking of not going to Duke."

"Because of Declan?"

"Why are we whispering?" Maria asked.

"I don't know, you started it."

Maria shrugged, cleared her throat, and returned to her normal speaking voice. "Who knows? Maybe because she doesn't want to go by herself without knowing anyone. It probably sounded exciting when she thought Declan was going too, but now that he's not...she's pissed."

"But Declan has to stay here because of his mom." Lizbet thought back to the accident a few weeks ago that had nearly severed Declan's mom's hand. Her doctors had said it was a miracle she was regaining use of it. But that accident had not only wounded Declan's mom, it had also caused a rift between Lizbet and Declan because Rufus, Gloria's dog, had warned her that Godwin, Declan's stepfather, would try to cause an accident in an attempt to kill Declan. Lizbet had successfully protected Declan, but not his mom. Lizbet tried not to blame herself for what had happened to Gloria, but her thoughts kept returning to that horrible day that changed everything. Her happiness at Declan's change of plans compounded her guilt. She took a deep breath and tried to refocus on Maria.

"I know that," Maria said. "Everyone knows that, including Nicole, but that doesn't mean she's happy about it. In fact, his willingness to stay with his mom after the accident just makes Declan look noble. And it makes Nicole look like a baby for not being brave enough to go alone."

"She should be able to change her mind." Lizbet hated sympathizing with Nicole, but she did anyway. She wasn't even sure if she wanted to travel across town to attend school, let alone across the country, far away from everyone she knew and loved.

"Yeah, but getting into a shouting and shoving match with someone three times her weight was just stupid."

Lizbet picked a bean off the vine and bit it in two. She thought while she munched. "Jason doesn't really seem like the type to let someone push him around."

"No, he doesn't, does he?" Maria used the back of her hand to push her dark hair off her forehead where a small string of sweat beads was starting to form. Half Latina and half Native American, Maria had an exotic beauty that even the early morning sun couldn't compete with. No wonder Baxter was crazy about her.

"Did you see the fight?" Lizbet asked.

"Everyone did. It happened right after you and Declan took off."

"Wow."

"I wonder if they'll both be at Sarah's bonfire tonight." Maria cocked her head at Lizbet. "You going to that?"

Lizbet buried her hand in the bush, grabbed a handful of beans, and yanked them off the vine. "Can't. I'm helping my mom. She has a gig at the yacht club."

"That's right. I forgot about that. Matias is working, too, right?" Maria slid Lizbet a look under her lashes. "How does Declan feel about you two working together?"

Lizbet flushed. "He's cool with it. Why wouldn't he be?"

"I love my brother, but I could see why Declan would feel differently. Did he seem okay with Jason kissing you last night?"

Lizbet laughed and picked up the basket of beans and balanced it on her hip as they reached the last bush in the row. "*I* wasn't okay with Jason kissing me last night... or ever."

Shooting hoops had been a lot more fun before Baxter's growth spurt had turned him into the jolly giant. There had been a time when Declan and Baxter had stood nose to nose, but that time had passed as Baxter had sprouted into a monster on the basketball court and an anomaly everywhere else. At the moment, he planted himself under the basketball hoop attached to his garage, snagged the ball from Declan, and casually tossed it in. Declan darted for the rebound and sprinted out of Baxter's considerable wingspan, knocking into McNally. McNally flew across the court, landed on his butt, and swore.

Declan froze, gaping at his friend. "Sorry, man." He hadn't even been aware of McNally behind him.

McNally stood, brushed himself off, and examined his arms and legs for bruises. His army of freckles accented his sweaty, flushed cheeks and his cowlick pointed to the sky as if standing in righteous indignation.

Baxter picked up the ball, tucked it under his arm, and scowled at Declan. "No need to throw punches.

Especially since he's on your team." Baxter, given his size, usually made up his own team.

Declan's gaze flinched between Baxter and McNally. "I didn't. I swear." He focused on McNally. "I didn't even know you were there."

"Sadly, that's what all the girls say as well..." McNally tried to make a joke of it.

The game resumed. McNally took the ball to the sideline and bounced it a few times before passing it to Declan. Baxter charged at Declan, but Declan darted across the court. Baxter followed but couldn't stop him. Declan jumped to sink the ball and kicked out his legs. His right foot made contact with Baxter's chest, sending Baxter sprawling onto his back.

McNally stared while the ball rolled across the court. "There's something seriously freaky going on."

"I don't know what you mean." Declan stared at Baxter who gazed blankly at the sky. "Are you okay?"

"Just let me catch...my breath." Baxter looked shell-shocked.

McNally pushed Declan. "You knocked the wind out of him!"

"Not intentionally! You know Baxter. He's harder to budge than Mount Rainier."

McNally peered at Baxter who lay with his legs curled into his chest.

"What did you do?" McNally pressed.

"I just...landed wrong... I'll be okay," Baxter sputtered.

Declan reached down to pull Baxter to his feet. Declan relaxed his grip and Baxter began flexing his hand as if it were aching.

"We're switching things up," Baxter said. "Me and you," he met McNally's gaze, "against him." He jerked a thumb in Declan's direction.

"It's on," McNally growled.

Baxter picked up the ball, thumped it against the concrete, and glared at Declan.

"Guys!" Declan began. "I didn't mean to—"

"Save your tears for your defeat," Baxter said through clenched teeth right before he rammed into Declan with his shoulder. Seconds later, Baxter was flat on the court.

"How did you do that?" McNally asked, looking genuinely confused. "I didn't even see you move."

"I didn't." Declan nodded at Baxter. "He did."

"How'd you flatten him?" McNally asked.

"He must have tripped." Declan chased after the ball, picked it up, and tucked it under his arm.

"No." McNally shook his head. "If he had tripped, he would have gone down face first, but he landed on his back. You must have pushed him!"

"He outweighs me by fifty pounds!"

Baxter groaned.

McNally crossed his arms and glowered. "Did you enroll in ninja classes?"

Declan held up his hands. "There's nothing ninja about me."

Baxter rolled onto his hands and knees like a dog, and hung his head.

McNally dropped into a squat beside him. "You all right?"

"Yeah," Baxter gasped. "I want an arm wrestling match."

"What?" Declan tried to laugh, but it sounded like a snort. "You've been whipping me at those since we were thirteen."

"I know." Baxter pushed himself to his feet. "There's something going on, but I don't get it. If you're taking steroids—why now? 'Cause you had to be clean during basketball season."

"Maybe he wants to try out for the UW team." McNally spoke as if Declan weren't there.

"Guys!" Declan tried not to be offended.

"It's not sex," McNally said. "Sex uses energy; it doesn't supply it."

"Oh, like you'd know!" Declan tossed the ball at McNally's chest. "Are we going to play or not?"

McNally caught the ball without ever taking his gaze off Declan.

Baxter eyed Declan. "So, are you and Lizbet?"

"I'm going to pretend this crazy conversation never happened." Declan knocked the ball out of McNally's hands and huffed off the court.

McNally caught up to him in two strides and grabbed his arm. Declan shook him off. McNally stared at his hand

as if Declan had stung him. Moments later, he planted himself in front of Declan. "What gives?"

Baxter joined him and folded his long arms across his enormous chest.

Declan pushed through their united front. "I don't know what you're talking about."

Stumbling backward, Baxter and McNally both fought to remain upright.

"It's drugs. It's gotta be drugs," Baxter murmured.

"Maybe he's just been working out," McNally said. "Nah...it doesn't work that fast, right?"

His friends trailed after Declan as he marched across the grass. Tickles, Baxter's dog, caught up to him and gave him a look that said he knew the answers to their questions.

Later, in the privacy of his bedroom, Declan set a goal to do as many push-ups as he could. During the basketball season, Coach Simmons routinely made the team do a hundred push-ups before each practice and Declan had generally blown through them. But he'd never set a goal to see how many he could do before his muscles failed. After about twenty minutes, he wished he had.

He quit when he could no longer stand the boredom, wondering what would have happened had he not stopped. Could he have really spent the day doing one push-up after another? While in school, he'd had access to the weights at the gym, but since school was out, he didn't have that option. Curiosity drove him to the closest sporting goods store to try out a weight set.

The Lake Lament Yacht Club sat at the eastern shore surrounded by thick woods and a sliver of gray beach. An unpretentious wooden building, it looked humbled by the glistening mighty boats docked along its moorings. The sun hovered on the distant shore and threatened to disappear into East End's shining skyline.

Lizbet wore what she considered her caterer's uniform: black shoes, hose, and skirt topped with a white button-down blouse. She kept her curls tied back with a black ribbon and tried to keep her lips pressed into a smile as the country-clubbers plucked the stuffed mushrooms and shrimp cocktails off her proffered tray.

Matias liked to make up stories and names for the yacht club members. "See the woman in the blue pantsuit? She's really Hillary Clinton's spy," Matias hissed as Lizbet headed to the kitchen to refill her tray.

"Why would Hillary have spies in East End?" she whispered back.

"Hillary has spies everywhere," he told her as he followed.

"Why? Is she planning a coup?" Lizbet plunked down her tray on the stainless-steel counter and began refilling it with a variety of appetizers.

Matias loaded his with sparkling drinks in dainty flutes. "She's not, but that man who looks like a walrus definitely is."

"There's a walrus here?" She picked up her tray and headed back out.

"You've seen him, right?" Matias once again followed. "He's hard to miss—or at least his mustache is. And the eyebrows. A grown person could get lost in the thickness of those eyebrows. That's probably where he hides the communication device."

Lizbet spotted the walrus-man and tried not to laugh. His eyebrows really did look like they could hide small animals.

"Of course, the scariest are the most ordinary."

"So that man in beige..." Lizbet whispered.

Matias nodded slowly. "Probably a Russian terrorist."

"And that woman in the white dress?"

"Definitely a member of the Mexican Mafia."

"But she's blonde and blue-eyed!"

"Good disguise, huh? I heard she paid a fortune for plastic surgery."

A tall redhead tapped her finger on Matias's arm. "I hope you're not gossiping about my guests!"

Matias had the grace to flush. "Uh, no. We're talking about my Aunt Freda."

The woman sniffed and melted a little beneath Matias's friendly smile. After she'd moved away, Lizbet whispered, "You don't have an Aunt Freda."

Matias let out a long sigh. "Poor Aunt Freda. She's always been invisible. No one ever notices her."

The redhead reached into her beaded bag as a phone

began to buzz. She slipped outside to take the call. She stood on the balcony on the other side of the wall-length window, her back to the room. Beyond her, the gray Puget Sound stretched to a pink horizon while gulls wheeled overhead.

Matias and Lizbet circled the room, offering their trays to the guests. Moments later, the redhead returned, looking shaken. She took a drink off Matias's tray and went to whisper to a man in beige pants and a dark blue dinner jacket.

"See, they're conspiring," Matias whispered.

Lizbet watched them. Something about their furtive exchange sent a chill down her spine. The couple moved outside to the deck and the woman tapped her phone again. Lizbet tried to watch them without being obvious. She sensed that something had happened to worry them. For her mom's sake, she hoped it had nothing to do with the catering. She glanced around the room at the guests and tried to eavesdrop on their conversations. A man with a distended belly was unhappy with the city mayor. A woman in a pink pantsuit had a daughter who wanted to quit a prestigious music school to join a rock band. Two men in dinner jackets were arguing about the state of the social security system. No one seemed unhappy with the food or the servers, and that was all Lizbet cared about.

When the couple who had taken the phone call disappeared, Lizbet kept an eye out for them. They didn't return, even after dinner was served. As they cleaned up, Lizbet had a chance to ask her mom about them.

"The Derringers?" Daugherty asked, her hands in a sink full of soapy water. "What do you want to know?"

"They disappeared before dinner was served. Weren't they the hosts? Don't you think that's odd?"

"Oh, maybe. They're busy people and own a number of businesses." Daugherty scrubbed a pan with a scouring pad. "Anything could have called them away."

Lizbet waited until the van was packed and the kitchen had been cleaned before she went to the deck where she'd seen the Derringers place their call. The sun had long since faded from view, and the moon left a streak of white on the silent Sound. The birds too had disappeared and she hoped they weren't already sleeping for the night. She reached into her pocket and pulled out a dinner roll. As soon as she started tearing it into small pieces, she had the attention of several gulls.

"Did I wake you?" she asked.

The gulls squawked at her in response.

She laughed. "I know you'd rather eat than sleep." She watched them gobble up the breadcrumbs for a moment before asking, "Did you hear or see anything strange tonight?"

"What do you mean?" a gull asked.

"I don't know." Lizbet really didn't know why she should care so much about one couple's telephone call. "Just anything off."

"Yes," one gull said.

"They didn't serve fish," another said. *"The yacht club almost always serve fish."*

"My mom told me Mrs. Derringer is allergic," Lizbet said. If the absence of a fish entre was as extraordinary as the evening got, Lizbet had nothing to worry about. Still, the knot of anxiety in her throat refused to unwind.

"That telephone call," another gull said.

"What about it?" Lizbet asked.

"It ended suddenly," the gull said.

"So, someone hung up without saying goodbye?" That wasn't so odd. Her aunt Josie almost never said goodbye and ended most phone conversations with a click.

"The person on the other end screamed," the gull said.

"Screamed?" Goosebumps rose on Lizbet's arms. "What did they say?"

The gull let out a loud squawk.

"So, they didn't say a word?"

SQUAWK!

Lizbet turned around to see Matias watching her with a funny look on his face.

"You look like you're holding court with these birds," he said.

"They like me because I give them leftovers." She showed him the partially eaten dinner roll in her hand.

"Everyone likes you," Matias said as he dropped a sweater around Lizbet's shoulders. "Ready to go?"

Lizbet really wanted to continue her discussion with the birds, but decided a telephone hang-up wasn't something she needed to worry about. Or was it?

"What's all this?" Gloria stood at the top of the basement stairs and frowned at the collection of boxes, weights, and pulleys gathered around Declan's feet.

"It's a Rock Solid 1500X weight machine," Declan said, glancing up from the instruction booklet. "It's mostly for me, but I thought it would be good for you, too."

"Mmm." Gloria frowned at him. "I lift weights at the physical therapist's office. I don't like it."

Declan smiled. "I don't think anyone does."

"So, why buy the machine?"

So that I can see how much I can bench press in the privacy of my basement, was what he thought. What he said was, "For the same reason I eat oatmeal."

Gloria laughed. "Okay, I get it. Just don't expect me to use it." She turned to leave. "And don't hurt yourself," she said over her shoulder.

Silence had its own music. Amplified, a void sucking in all the sounds that should have been: chattering squirrels, calling birds, the buzz of insects. Still. Dark. Silence as heavy as water.

Hunger burned the back of his throat and tightened his gut. He padded across the forest floor. A carpeting of pine needles and soft soil muffled his footfalls. Above

the trees' canopy, a smattering of stars glistened, pale against a cloud-filled night. Mist shrouded the round, full strawberry moon.

He sat back on his haunches and lifted his head toward the moon. Snatches of conversations drifted by. *The girl must die... He's young, unskilled...not used to our ways.*

His ears twitched. The voices...they belonged to the wind. Or did they? Who was the girl spoken of? Could it be Lizbet?

Her name sent ripples of apprehension through his blood. He gazed at his paw...so foreign. How had he transformed into this creature? Standing on all fours, he loped through the woods aimlessly, fighting the hunger that zinged through his veins. He came to a clearing at the top of a hill and shuddered to a stop in a circle of stones. This place... Lizbet had told him of this place.

Again, her name sent a shiver of dread down his spine. Those voices on the wind...they meant Lizbet. She couldn't be dead. He would know. He would feel her death as certainly as he would feel his own. He turned and ran.

His speed amazed him. He tore through the woods at lightning speed, the trees flashing by, his paws barely touching the ground. Power surged through his flanks. A feeling of invincibility coursed through him. Moments later he paused beneath the tree beside the farmhouse and gazed up at Lizbet's window, willing her to join him in the moonlight. He called her name, but all that came out was a whimper.

Chapter 3

He woke as before—shivering in the cold morning light. The brand new sun didn't have warmth to spare. The remains of his pants clung to a branch of a cedar tree, strips of his shirt littered the ferns on the forest floor, and one sandal hung near a robin's nest high in a birch...the other...he couldn't see the other one.

He really liked those sandals.

He needed help. And not just because he didn't want to replace his wardrobe every month...every month? When was his last nightmare? As he gathered up the remains of his clothes, his jumbled thoughts skittered over the past few days and weeks. Had there been a full moon last night?

He couldn't think this way. This line of thought had to stop. He didn't believe in werewolves.

And yet, he had seen one with his own eyes.

And he was in love with the girl who could talk to animals.

Lizbet came downstairs the next morning to find her mother fidgeting in the kitchen. Lizbet could tell from the crease between her mom's eyebrows that something bothered her. Slight, fair, and pink-cheeked, Daugherty was opposite in nearly every way to Lizbet. Which made more sense now that she knew she wasn't her mother's biological daughter. But it took more than blood to make a family, and Lizbet could read her mother's moods like a magazine.

She wrapped her arms around Daugherty's waist and laid her head on her mom's shoulder. "Something wrong?"

Daugherty took her time before answering as if weighing her words to measure the pain they could deliver. "The Derringer girl didn't come home last night."

The anxious knot in Lizbet's spine tightened. "Why?"

"No one knows. Elsa got a call from Courtney in the middle of the party. Courtney screamed and dropped the phone and that's the last anyone has heard from her."

"Strange." Lizbet pulled away from her mom, plucked the coffee mug from Daugherty's fingers, and refilled it before filling a mug for herself.

"So strange." Daugherty plopped into a kitchen chair and began to drum her fingers on the table.

Lizbet placed the loaded coffee mug in front of her mom. "So many weird things are happening around here..." She

sat in a chair on the opposite side of the table and took a sip of coffee while watching her mom over the rim of her mug.

"Declan's grandfather and those wolves..." Daugherty sipped her own coffee.

Lizbet nodded, knowing her mom only knew a fraction of the weirdness blowing around East End. "And then that attorney just disappeared. Leo Cabriolet."

Daugherty slammed her mug onto the table causing the coffee to slosh over the rim. "Yes! What was that about?"

Lizbet shrugged even though she knew that werewolf was dead. "According to Declan's mom, the police think he's in cahoots with Godwin."

"And they still can't find him. I can't believe a man can just go off the grid in today's technological world."

But Lizbet knew it would be really hard to find a wolf if you thought you were looking for a man.

Daugherty shook her head as if trying to clear it of all the puzzles. "What do you have going on today?"

"Remember? Declan and I are going to Blackstone Island to see if we can find anything more about Rose."

"That's right. You told me you were going to do that." Daugherty blew out a sigh. "I really wish I had more I could tell you. That whole episode still feels unreal. I'm so sorry I'm such a blank slate. Memories from those twenty years are like TV reruns of a show I didn't even particularly like."

Lizbet patted her mom's hand. "You had amnesia. You shouldn't apologize for that."

"I know, but still..."

"It must be so strange to have lost almost half of your life."

"I'd rather lose twenty years than a daughter." The worry wrinkle between Daugherty's brows returned. "I'm just sick for the Derringers. They must be out of their minds with worry."

A knock at the door interrupted them. Lizbet turned to wave Declan inside. His eyes were red-rimmed, and he looked...off, but she couldn't say why. Also, his shirt strained against his chest as if he'd gained weight. Not just weight, but muscles...lots of them. He looked healthy, but tired. Her thoughts went back to the book on sleep he'd picked up at the bookstore. She'd have to ask him about that. But not in front of her mom. "Ready to go?" she asked.

He tried to smile back, but his expression, like his shirt, looked strained. "Yeah."

Daugherty twisted in her chair and pushed a weary hand through her hair. "Do you know Courtney Derringer?"

Caution flickered in his eyes. "She was a year behind me in school. Why?"

"She's missing," Lizbet said.

Declan paled. "Missing? How?"

"She didn't come home last night," Daugherty told him.

The tension in Declan's eyes softened. "That could mean anything."

"There's more to it than that. Her parents are frantic." Daugherty told him the same thing she'd told Lizbet. "If you hear anything, let me know."

"Sure." Declan flipped the keys in his hands. "But she's probably just bunked out at someone's house." His words sounded casual and relaxed, but the worried wrinkle between his eyebrows didn't fade away until they were out on the water, the sea breeze blowing them westward.

The birds and dolphins sent greetings as Declan powered his boat into the small harbor of the island where Lizbet had spent the first seventeen years of her life. Lizbet waved in return, calling the animals by name.

Her heart lifted as it always did whenever she returned to Blackstone Island, even though her expectations were low. "Remember how we found very little about Rose the last time we were here," she said as she helped Declan tie the boat up to the tiny dock.

"We're looking for different things this time." Declan straightened and gazed up the path leading to the house that Lizbet had called home. "I still can't believe you lived here like hermits. This place looks like it could belong to rabbits."

"It does, sort of." Ivy had overrun the house, making it look more like a bush than a structure. "I think the foliage was part of the camouflage. Poor Rose. Imagine trying to hide for so many years."

Declan elbowed her. "Come on. Let's go see what we can find."

Lizbet's feet faltered as they climbed through the gorse and tall grass. A smattering of clouds filled the mid-morning sky and the cool wind carried a hint of rain. "It seems fruitless."

"Not necessarily," Declan said. "Last time, you were just looking for anything about your mom. This time, we want not only that, but also recipes and any hint of her ancestry, especially your father—including her dealings with werewolves."

"Werewolves?" She paused at the low stone wall that surrounded the house. "I don't think Rose was a werewolf."

"Why not?" Declan placed his hand on the small of her back to guide her up the walkway. "Leo Cabriolet was and we think Godwin could be. Why not Rose?"

Lizbet slid Declan a quick glance. His voice had that casual overstressed tone again. "Are there such things as female werewolves?"

"Why not? Every other species has both sexes. It would be weird if there weren't."

"Oh, yeah, that's what's weird."

He grinned. "Okay, so there's plenty of weirdness to go around..."

"You betcha."

Declan bit his lip as if he wanted to say something.

Lizbet climbed the steps leading to the front porch and pulled a string of keys from her pocket. "A lock on this door is just one of the weird-oddities."

"You didn't ever lock the door when you lived here?"

"Why would we? No one ever came here."

"That's not true. My dad came here. Godwin came here."

"Well, your dad was definitely invited, although Godwin

wasn't." Lizbet scrunched her forehead in thought. "Maybe Rose figured that if someone was already on the island it would be pointless to try and lock them out. Although, it's possible that if she were like me and could communicate with the animals she probably felt she didn't need one. The animals are a better security system than money can buy or man can make."

"That's for sure," Declan said.

"You're thinking about Leroy, aren't you?"

"Who?"

"Leroy, the bear?"

"It's so weird you're on a first-name basis with bears."

"But handy."

Lizbet pushed open the door and a wave of wistful longing swept over her. Of course, she'd never trade her earlier lonely life for the one she had now—the boy next to her being the most important reason—but in many ways life on the island had been easier, less complicated, and sweeter. Her gaze swept over the stacks of books. "We're looking for cookbooks and anything relating to legends and myths."

"There's like a thousand books in this room."

Lizbet sighed and settled down cross-legged in front of the shelves lining the far wall. "Isn't it wonderful?"

Declan left Lizbet in the living room and went to inspect the office.

"There's just gardening books in there," Lizbet called after him.

"It won't hurt to double check," he told her. The office held a desk, a chair, and a massive bookshelf. After scanning the agricultural books, *Composting 101, Living Off the Land and Loving It, Dirt Farming for Dummies,* he realized that Lizbet had been right. He sat in the chair and looked around the room. He was missing something.

Declan gazed at the large painting on the wall opposite the window. It was a picture of a farmhouse surrounded by pastures full of fluffy white sheep. A pastoral, his mom would call it. It seemed off somehow. Not quite centered on the wall and slightly askew. He stood to straighten it, and it fell into his hands, revealing a recessed bookshelf built into the wall. Here were the books he needed. *The History of Monsters and Their Mayhem, Shape Shifters—Heroes or Demons? The Truth about Wolves, Summoning Shifters, Vampire Realities, From the Shadows: True Tales of Dark Creatures, Taming the Monster Within, Immortal Magic.*

Feeling slightly sick, Declan propped the painting against the wall and went in search of a box to carry his find.

They took a break at noon and opened the lunch Daugherty had prepared for them.

"Want to take it outside?" Declan asked.

"Sure. Let me get a quilt." With the basket of food in one hand and a blanket tucked under her arm, Lizbet led Declan through the back door. "There's a killer view at the top of the hill."

It made her sad to walk past her mom's neglected vegetable garden. The berries had taken over, creating a tangle of sticker brambles, although a few pumpkin vines had managed to survive.

Declan took the blanket, spread it out, and settled onto it. Lizbet sat beside him with her legs crossed. While they ate, they talked about the books they'd found. Lizbet's biggest prize was a collection of cookbooks that looked more like spells than recipes.

"Want to try them?" Lizbet asked, sliding onto his lap.

"Yeah, but..." Indecision flared in Declan's eyes.

"Is something wrong?" She kissed the side of his jaw and trailed her lips down his neck.

"You're talking about the recipes, right?" He audibly swallowed.

"Partly." She pulled away from him so she could look in his eyes. "Why? What did you think I was asking about?" She grinned and ran her hands over his chest.

He audibly swallowed again. "Lizbet..."

"We're completely alone here. No one can interrupt us."

Declan gently lifted her off his lap and climbed to his feet.

Lizbet stared at him, upset and confused. "It's too soon?"

Declan ran his fingers through his hair and stared out at the water.

"It's okay... I'm sorry." Lizbet jumped up and shook out the blanket, trying to look busy so he couldn't see how much his rejection hurt.

"Lizbet." He wrapped his arms around her and pulled her against his chest. "I would love...you don't even know how much, but I..."

"What's wrong?" She laced her fingers through his. "I thought you wanted this..."

"I do, but—" He groaned. "What if I'm a werewolf?" The words tumbled out in a rush.

"What?" She stepped away from him.

"I've had these crazy...dreams."

"Dreams?" She studied his face. She knew the shape of his cheeks, the angle of his jaw, but she didn't recognize the uneasiness in his eyes.

"Okay. They seem like they're more than dreams. And they coincide with the full moon."

"How many dreams?"

"Two. One last month and then another last night."

"But dreams are just dreams. They could mean anything, right?" She waved her hand around. "Dreams are craziness."

"But when I wake up—outside, I might add—my clothes are shredded. And I'm naked. In the woods. It's super awkward...and creepy."

Lizbet blinked. "You can't be a werewolf. You're too nice. Only—"

"We don't know how it works."

"No, we don't." She pushed against him. "What does that have to do with…you know?" She slid her hand under his shirt, liking the warmth of his skin, enjoying that she made him shiver.

He stepped away from her. "What if it's hereditary? Some of my reading suggests that it is."

She edged toward him as if he were a frightened animal that she had to sneak up on. "You've been reading legends? Those aren't real!"

"How do we know what's real and what's not? What if it's spread like AIDS?" He held up his hands to ward her off.

"Are you going to tell me that we can't even kiss?" She took two steps away from him. "Do you honestly intend to remain celibate your entire life?"

"My entire life?" His eyes sought hers. "No. But until I understand what's happening to me, yes."

"What if Godwin's my father?"

"Don't even think that."

"Well, he could be, right? We know—or at least suspect—that Rose was hiding from her abusive husband. If Godwin was Rose's ex, that means he was probably my father."

"I don't believe it."

"And that would make me half werewolf."

"No."

They stared at each other. After a moment, Lizbet came

to peace with his decision. She leaned into him and laid her head against his chest and listened to his heart beating. "You're not a werewolf. I'm sure of it." She glanced at the sky and spotted the silvery edge of daylight moon hiding behind a shroud of dark clouds. "And neither am I."

Declan glanced through the basement window. A few stars pin-pricked the purpling sky and the sun skimmed the tops of the trees. Soon the moon would rise. He stretched out on a sleeping bag with his cell phone tucked between his ear and shoulder. Beside him lay the stack of books that he'd taken from Blackstone Island.

"Are you sure you don't want me to stay?" Lizbet's voice floated through the phone.

"The farther away you are the safer you are." He'd already dead-bolted the door.

"I'm not worried about my safety."

"You should be." Declan frowned at the sky again. He'd told his mom he was staying at his dad's and his dad he was staying at his mom's, when in actuality he was spending the night locked in the basement of his stepfather's deserted house. A mean wind moaned through the windows and occasionally the house creaked like an old man with achy bones.

"It's craziness," Lizbet said.

"It's an experiment. There's surveillance cameras all over this place, and a deadbolt on the door. I'm seven miles from town and two acres away from the closest neighbor."

He was completely alone. Except for the mouse. Declan watched the tiny creature sit back on its haunches and peer at him with pink eyes. "Did you send a mouse to spy on me?" he asked Lizbet.

Her silence answered his question.

"What's he going to do? He's a mouse!"

"He's well connected."

"Meaning he's going to rat me out to his animal friends who will make sure I behave?"

"I'm not sure Rapscallion has many friends."

"Rapscallion? He has a name?"

"Of course he has a name!"

"I'll see you tomorrow, okay?"

Her voice softened. "Be safe."

"I'm not worried about my safety," he said again before saying goodbye and ending the call.

Declan tried to ignore Rapscallion as he fluffed his pillow and settled down with a book entitled *The History of Monsters and Their Mayhem*. He flipped it open and turned to the Chapter on werewolves.

Werewolves are shape-shifting creatures that have both fascinated and terrified man since the beginning of time. The werewolf legend covers the globe with sightings recorded in ancient Greece,

China, Iceland, and South America. Where the legend actually began and where and when it may end can only be speculated.

Like the famed witch trials, there are numerous accounts of suspected werewolves being hunted, questioned and executed. Perhaps some were accused because villagers needed a scapegoat to hold accountable for the deaths of their livestock, but many others were charged for far more sinister reasons.

In 1521, Pierre Burgot and Michel Verdun were tried and executed in France for being werewolves. In reality, they were a team of serial killers, but their cooperation fed the legend's flame of wolves working together in a pack with supernatural telepathic abilities. Gilles Garnier, also known as the Werewolf of Dole, was another confessed serial killer.

A German man, Peter Stumpp, was reportedly apprehended by his neighbors in his wolf form. Stumpp confessed to murder, rape, and cannibalism, but refused to demonstrate his use of his "wolf-girdle." But these are not the first recorded instances of werewolves and their crimes.

Metamorphoses, written in 1 A.D. by Ovid, tells the tale of King Lycaon (the origin of the word lycanthrope) who offended the gods by serving human meat to them at a banquet. Jupiter punished this transgression by transforming Lycaon into a werewolf. In his

werewolf form, he could continue his abomination of eating human flesh with less offense. In this early rendition, the werewolves changed shape at will. It's only in later legends that the moon plays a role in the transformations. Other tales tell of a belt or "wolf-girdle" that would change them.

Religion, too, played a role in the evolving myth. In a Christian community, any shape-shifting was considered witchcraft. It was believed that the wolf-girdle was a satanic tool provided to men by the devil or his minions to tempt men to be their very worst selves.

There are many suppositions for the appearance of the werewolf myth. There was a time when most of the world was overrun with packs of wolves. There is also the possibility that the myth stemmed from rabies.

Just as a rabid animal will appear to go wild, people who develop furious rabies will be hyperactive and excitable and display erratic behavior. Symptoms include insomnia, anxiety, confusion, agitation, hallucinations, and excessive salivation.

Feeling sick, Declan swallowed, put down the book, stared out the window at the rising moon, and waited.

Chapter 4

Birdsong. A sharp wind pricking his skin. Declan's eyes fluttered open. He knew he shouldn't be surprised to find himself buck-naked in the woods—he had prepared for this possibility—but still... He didn't think he could ever get used to waking in the woods naked. It could be worse...maybe one morning he'd find himself on a city sidewalk, or in the fast lane of the interstate, or on the steps of the city courthouse. Pushing himself into a sitting position, he rolled his shoulders and sought landmarks in the forest—anything that might tell him where he was, and how far he was from where he'd stashed his clothes.

He was lying in a bed of ferns that kept him marginally modest as long as he was sitting. Standing would be another story. He thought of Adam and Eve and their strategically placed grape leaves. He glanced around at the ferns, pines and cedars. Where was a maple leaf when he needed it?

The wind ruffled his hair and a chill passed over his skin. He wanted to tell the birds to be quiet so he could hear the noises that had woken him. Staying low, he edged behind a large blackberry bush, being careful to not stand too close so as not to be pricked. Never had a blackberry bush seemed so dangerous. As he drew near the clearing, he saw red and blue lights flashing in the murky, predawn air.

An ambulance was parked on the street in front of a craftsman-style home. The front door opened and a pair of EMTs rolled a gurney out the front door. A body lay beneath a blood-soaked white sheet.

Adrenaline coursed through Declan. No longer concerned for his modesty, he dashed through the forest to find his clothes. His sense of smell guided him to where he'd stashed his sneakers, T-shirt, boxers and jeans. He threw them on, but ditched his shoes when he heard the ambulance rumble to life. He sprinted after the ambulance, but took care to stay in the shelter of the trees. The thought that he should be wary of where he stepped came to him, but it didn't slow him down. Trees and bushes whipped past as he matched the pace of the ambulance with ease.

He had to know who lay inside on the gurney. The fear that he had killed someone clutched his throat, making his breath ragged and labored.

Lizbet climbed on her motorbike and sped to Godwin's house as soon as the sun rose in the east. She propped her bike up against the stone pillars and scaled the wrought-iron gate. After landing hard on her feet, she ran for the side of the house. She peered in all the basement windows, and while she saw Declan's crumpled sleeping bag and smashed pillow, she could not see him, so she tried knocking on the doors and windows, calling his name.

"Lizbet." He appeared behind her, bare-chested, wearing only a pair of low-slung jeans. His hair was wild and a streak of blood smeared his arm.

"Oh Declan!" She flung herself against him. "Are you all right?" She ran her hand across the streak of blood, but couldn't see or feel a corresponding wound "Where'd this come from?"

He gave a small, almost imperceptible shake of his head. "I don't know."

"What happened?"

"I don't know that either."

"At least you're dressed."

"Sort of. I planted these pants at the edge of the woods."

"So there's a pile of shredded clothes in the forest?"

"No. I slept naked."

"Oh." She grinned, although she knew he wouldn't find any of this in any way amusing. "That was smart."

"Yeah. I didn't want to have to restock my closet every month." He edged her toward the house. "Come on, let's go inside. I'm starving."

"That's probably good, right?"

"What do you mean?"

"You're starving...that means you haven't eaten."

He shook his head again. "I don't know what it means." He led her up the steps to the back porch. After retrieving a key hidden on top of the doorframe and twisting it in the lock, he pulled open the Dutch door.

"Did you..." she started.

"Did I what?" he asked when she didn't finish her question. He paused in the mudroom and tried to wipe off the dirt and blades of grass clinging to his bare feet.

She swallowed and slipped off her shoes. "I'm sure this had nothing to do with...what just happened to you."

"What?" he pressed.

She followed him into the kitchen and watched as he pulled a frying pan from the cupboard and fetched some eggs from the fridge. He frowned at the carton. "Do eggs go bad? These have to be weeks old."

"I don't know. Can you look it up on your phone?"

"My phone is in the basement." Setting down the eggs and spatula, he headed for the basement.

He'd be back any minute. He'd turn on his phone and see the news. Or would he? Lizbet shuddered with a deep sigh and sat down at the table. She couldn't hide this from him, but she also couldn't let him believe that he would have had anything to do with this...because that was exactly what he would think. But she knew he would never kill anyone. Even if he was a wolf.

"You don't remember anything that happened last night?" she asked when he reappeared.

"No." He cracked all the eggs in the frying pan.

"That must be strange."

"Not really, if you think about it." He pointed his spatula at her. "It's not as if you can remember what you're doing when you're asleep."

"So, it's like being asleep?"

He nodded and stirred his eggs.

"You're going to eat eight eggs?"

His hand froze above the pan. "You don't want any?"

"I might want one or two, max. Definitely not five."

"I might as well eat them. According to the Internet, they shouldn't last more than five weeks."

"And the bacon? How long will it last?"

He shook his head. "Doesn't matter. I'm going to eat it as soon as it's fried." He poised the spatula over the frying pan. "Jason Norbit is dead," he said without looking at her.

She nodded. "I know. But I also know it wasn't you."

"You. Don't. Know. That." He spoke slowly. "I heard the EMTs say he was attacked by what appears to have been a large dog." He placed his hand on his chest. "I'm a large dog."

"No. You're not."

"I absolutely am. You can watch the surveillance videos to prove it, if you wish. I already did."

She jumped to her feet. "Declan, you have to get rid of the videos! What if your mom or the police find them?"

He hung his head. "I know. I wanted to show you...to prove to you that I'm not safe."

She crossed the room in two steps, wrapped her arms around his waist and laid her head on his back. "I'm not afraid of you."

"You should be."

"You need to destroy those videos. They aren't going to tell us anything about Jason."

"How do you know that?"

She opened her mouth, but couldn't find the words to make a solid argument. She held up a finger. "Wait a minute. Rapscallion!"

Declan looked at her as if she were the crazy one. He frowned when a fat little mouse crawled out of the cupboard and jumped onto the counter.

Lizbet fished in her pocket and pulled out a square of cheese. "Gouda," she told the mouse. "Good stuff from the Netherlands."

The mouse's whiskers twitched with anticipation.

"Did you do as I asked?"

Rapscallion nodded and cast Declan a frightened glance.

"And what happened?"

"Squee! *He turned into a wolf.*"

"What did he say?" Declan asked.

"You're a wolf," she told him.

Declan didn't look surprised, but his shoulders still sagged. "I can't live as a wolf!"

"You're only a wolf three nights out of every month!"

"What if I killed Jason?" He put down his spatula and met her gaze. "Lizbet—you hated me when you thought I could exterminate him." He waved at the mouse. "How are you going to feel about me when you learn I killed a man? I can't stomach it..."

"Stop it. You didn't kill Jason!"

"How do you know? I woke near his house! I saw the police cars and ambulance. I watched them load him into the coroner's van. I had to make my way home—naked— through the woods without being seen!" He pointed at his chest. "I don't even know whose blood this is!"

Lizbet stared at the muscles rippling across his torso. She couldn't meet his eyes. "That's bad."

"Yeah. I can't live with this."

She bounced from her chair to take both his hands in hers. "You have to! There isn't an alternative."

"Really? Because I can think of a few." He sucked in a deep breath. "You said you cured Tickles."

"I'm not going to feed you silver dust and raw meat. It's too dangerous."

"Oh—and running through the woods and killing people isn't dangerous?"

"Stop it." She slapped his arm. "You did not kill Jason."

"What about the other girl? Courtney Derringer. I probably killed her, too."

"No. I don't believe it. They say that a person under hypnosis wouldn't do anything that breaks their moral code and being under hypnosis is probably a lot like being a werewolf."

"Declan the teenager has a high moral code, but how do I know what kind of animal Declan the wolf is? Do you think wolves are vegetarians?" He scooped out the eggs onto two plates, pulled two forks from the silverware drawer, and sat down at the kitchen table. He pointed his fork at her. "You have to do to me whatever it is you did to Tickles." He took a few bites of eggs and chewed on the bacon. "Could I talk to him?"

She blinked. "You could try, I guess." She watched Declan shoveling his breakfast into his mouth. Carefully, as if the plate were fragile, she picked it up and sat down at the table. Studying him, she tried to imagine how he must be feeling. Worried. Guilt stricken. Confused. She was all of those things, too.

Lizbet pushed her eggs around her plate, trying to summon up hope or at least an appetite. As hard as it was to believe that Declan could be a werewolf, she found it even harder to believe that he could have anything to do with Jason's death or Courtney's disappearance.

After Declan showered and dressed, he got on the back of Lizbet's motorbike and rode with her to Baxter's house. If Mrs. Dresden was surprised to see him so early in the morning, she was even more surprised when Declan asked if he could take Tickles for a walk. She wore a fluffy pink bathrobe and a pair of furry bunny slippers. Tickles wiggled beside her, wagging his stub of a tail.

"I was hard on Baxter the other day on the basketball court so I thought I'd make it up to him by doing his chore," Declan lied.

Mrs. Dresden blinked. "That's really kind of you, but you must know that Baxter hasn't taken Tickles on a walk for at least a year."

"Well, then he probably really wants to go, don't you, boy?" Declan knelt beside the Schnauzer and rubbed between his ears. Tickles whimpered.

Mrs. Dresden raised her eyebrows. "It's hard to argue with altruism. Just a minute, let me find his leash."

Baxter shuffled down the hall wearing a pair of Star Wars pajamas and a white T-shirt. He looked rumpled and sleepy. "What are you doing here?" he asked.

"Walking your dog," Declan replied.

"Why?"

"It's *National Walk-a-Dog Day*." Declan fondled Tickles' ears and wouldn't meet Baxter's eyes.

"Then why aren't you walking your own dog?" Baxter asked with a smirk.

"Who says I didn't?" Declan straightened. "Do you have a problem with me walking your dog?"

"Yeah. It's weird." Baxter shrugged. "But it's your picnic. I'm sure Tickles won't mind."

But the dog did mind.

"I don't really want to talk about that painful episode," Tickles told Lizbet as soon as they were away from the house and in the shelter of the woods.

"But the cure worked, right?" Lizbet pressed.

"Yes, it did. Sort of."

"What's he saying?" Declan asked.

"What do you mean, 'sort of'?" Lizbet asked the dog.

He gave a doggy version of a shrug. *"Maybe it worked, maybe it didn't. Because of the electric fence, I no longer leave the property, but sometimes I still find myself outside in the morning without knowing how I got there."*

"He still has episodes that he can't explain," Lizbet told Declan. "But he knows he doesn't leave the property because of the electric fence."

"Great. All I need is an electric fence." Declan stared out at the trees and lifted his chin. "I still want to try it."

"Fine. I'll make it, but you can't eat it until you're a wolf." Lizbet stopped beneath a giant maple tree.

"What are we going to do all day while we wait?" Declan and Tickles stood beside her. No one seemed to know where to go or what to do.

"We should try to figure out if there's any connection between Jason's death and Courtney's disappearance," Lizbet said, but she didn't know where to begin.

Tickles looked from one to the other. *"Why don't you join Courtney's search party? That's what I would do if I were you. But take me home first."*

The mid-afternoon sun backlit the tops of the grove of aspen trees. The tall yellow grass pricked Lizbet's legs as she and Declan waded toward the patrol car parked at the edge of the woods near Carlton Field. There were police officers, firefighters, and a collection of community volunteers. Many had dogs on leashes and a few carried rifles. Overhead, drones flew, skimming the tops of the trees.

"We should have brought Rufus," Lizbet whispered. The guns made her nervous. Why bring them? Was everyone as concerned about the wolves as she was? Or did they think the kidnapper was still around?

Declan put his hand to his forehead.

"What's wrong? Are you okay?" Lizbet asked, worrying about his pale color and the faraway look in his eyes.

He shook like a dog trying to shake off water.

"What is it?"

"So weird," he muttered. "My sense of smell...it's making me nuts." He put his hands on both sides of his head. "I'm going insane."

Lizbet wrapped her arm around his waist and tried to steer him away from the woods and fields. "We don't have to do this. We can just go home."

Declan shook himself again. "No. I want to be here. I want to help. I have to know…"

"Your heightened senses should be an advantage, right?"

He blinked, and told her about his basketball game with Baxter and McNally and his increased strength.

"Maybe there's an upside to being a monster," Lizbet said.

A slight man with a German Shepherd on a very short leash climbed from a Range Rover and also headed toward the patrol car. The dog spotted Lizbet and whimpered. *"I don't want to be on this leash."*

She sent him a sympathetic glance.

"I want to run. Why won't he let me run?"

Lizbet ran her hand over the dog's head. "He's beautiful," she told the man.

"He's really strong," the man said, tightening his hold on the leash. "I keep telling my wife he'll be more manageable as he matures, but it's not happening."

"How old is he?" Lizbet asked.

"Nearly two."

Lizbet smiled. "He's a teenager and you know what they say about those."

The man grinned. "You're a teenager, right? I don't see you bucking on a leash."

"Oh, I definitely would if anyone tried to put one on me." Lizbet scratched the fur between the dog's ears.

"You're a good boy, huh?" she addressed the dog.

He whimpered. *"It doesn't matter how good I am, I never get treats."*

"Have you tried giving him Cheerios?" Lizbet asked the man. "Dogs love Cheerios."

The man snorted. "I don't want to make him fat!"

Lizbet sent the teen-dog another sympathetic look as the man pulled on the leash.

The search party had obviously been in full force for a number of hours, but the officer standing near the patrol car looked pleased to see them. "Nicole Gunner last saw Courtney Derringer in this vicinity. We have an article of her clothing—" He held up a letterman jacket for the German Shepherd to smell.

Beside her, Declan flinched and Lizbet noticed.

"What is it?" Lizbet whispered as soon as they were alone in the woods.

"The letterman jacket, it's Nicole's."

"Are you sure? How can you tell? It looked like she had a tennis patch."

"They're both on the tennis team. Or they were, but the smell..."

"Maybe they both wore the same perfume, or used the same shampoo."

Declan shook his head. "No. That smell. It belongs to just Nicole."

She slid him a sideways glance. "It's kind of creepy you know that. How do I smell?"

He grinned. "Like something I want to eat really, really badly."

She stopped and stared at him. A shaft of sunlight broke through the trees' canopy and landed on his hair. "Really?"

"Really, really."

"Well, please don't."

He grinned and turned and marched toward a grove of aspens. As they walked, the grove of aspens began to thin. A rugged path snaked along the edge of the cliff that lined the acres of swamp.

"Declan?" Lizbet asked. "Are you intentionally heading toward the slough?"

"Seems like a good place to hide a body," Declan said.

Lizbet shivered as she studied the thick marsh when they reached the edge of the cliff. A sheer thirty-foot drop marked with rocks and clusters of ferns bordered the slough. Small streams cut through the wetland's patches of pussy willows and reeds. Ducks floated in the brackish water, and Lizbet noted several beaver dams.

Above her, a squirrel chattered. Lizbet glanced around. No one else seemed to be in earshot. "Hello," she called to the squirrel. "We're looking for a missing girl." She paused, realizing that she didn't even know what Courtney looked like. She elbowed Declan. "Describe her."

Declan stared at the squirrel. "Are you telling me he can understand me?"

"Of course *she* can."

"*She* speaks English?"

"No. She chatters." Lizbet folded her arms. "How did you think I communicate with them?"

"I don't know. I guess I thought it was telepathic."

"Telepathic? That's just silly."

Declan raised his eyebrows. "Silly is no longer relevant. Anything is possible."

She considered him. "Maybe so." She nudged him again. "Go ahead, describe Courtney."

"She's tall, has reddish-brown hair, and she usually wears tennis shorts."

Lizbet smirked. "The squirrel doesn't know what tennis shorts are."

A sudden low growling stopped their argument. A patch of diffused morning light shone through the canopy of trees, illuminating the unruly German Shepherd they had seen earlier. He stood erect with his head lowered and his tail pointing straight behind him. His vicious stance made him both terrible and beautiful. Men, guns, and barking dogs followed. The fur on the back of the German Shepherd's neck rose like a mohawk as he lunged toward the squirrel.

Lizbet stood helplessly at the edge of the cliff watching the slight man try to control his dog. Someone bumped her from behind.

On her descent over the cliff, Lizbet felt nothing but surprise on finding herself airborne. She called for help, but the report of a shotgun drowned out her voice. Her hands frantically clutched at the ferns and rocks protruding from the cliff wall as she sailed past, but nothing stopped her fall until she smacked into something large, warm, and furry.

Chapter 5

Above her, a woman screamed.

The German Shepherd barked like he'd treed a raccoon and bucked on his leash while his master swore and fought for control.

"Lizbet!" Declan called as he started to scramble down the incline.

Two burly men each grabbed one of his arms.

"Don't do it, son," a man in a black and white flannel shirt said.

Lizbet glanced up at the big black bear holding her gently in his arms. "I'm okay, Leroy, you can put me down," she whispered.

The creature carefully set her on the ground. The loose dirt slipped beneath her feet and she grabbed a nearby huckleberry bush to stop her from sliding any farther.

Leroy roared and those gathered at the cliff's edge all flinched. A man raised his gun.

"Don't shoot! You'll hit the girl!" a woman cried.

"I'm okay," Lizbet called to the crowd above. "I'm not even hurt."

She felt Leroy's gaze on her back as she scrambled up the hill.

The man with the gun at his shoulder took aim at the bear. Lizbet grabbed the gun barrel and pointed it at the ground. "Don't be stupid," she said through clenched teeth while Leroy disappeared into a thicket of trees.

Declan grabbed her and folded her into his arms. "What happened?"

"I don't know," she mumbled into his shirt. "Someone knocked into me."

"On purpose?" He pulled away from her to gaze into her eyes while running his hands over her arms.

She shrugged, feeling sick and shaky.

"That bear." A woman pushed forward and pulled a tiny notepad and a pencil out of her breast pocket. "He saved you. Remarkable."

"Yes," Lizbet said, trying to sound as surprised as the people gathered around her.

"Did you have any prior experience with him?" the woman with the pad and pencil asked.

Lizbet blinked at the woman and tried to come up with a response. "How could I?"

"Maybe he was trained or domesticated...somehow," the woman pressed.

"Not by me!" A nervous giggle escaped Lizbet's lips.

"Those Russian dancing bears are supposed to be really tame," the man with the German Shepherd said.

"You can't even control your dog," a man in a black cowboy hat scoffed. "What makes you think you could tame a bear?"

"I didn't say I was going to tame a bear," the man said. "I'm just saying not all bears are vicious."

Declan ran his hands over Lizbet as if searching for broken bones or torn skin. "Let's go," he said in her ear.

Lizbet's Aunt Josie slammed through the front door, and shook her finger at Lizbet and Declan sitting on the living room sofa before stomping into the kitchen. Declan raised his eyebrows in question. Lizbet answered with a shrug. Moments later, raised voices came from the next room.

Josie emerged and Elizabeth, wringing her hands in her apron, followed.

"Tell me about the bear." Josie planted herself in front of Lizbet and crossed her skinny arms. Even though it was Saturday, Josie still wore a business suit, as if she had a board meeting to attend.

Lizbet and Declan exchanged glances.

"It was no biggie," Lizbet said.

A vein in Josie's neck throbbed. "That's not what I heard."

"I didn't hear anything about this," Elizabeth said, and she settled down in the La-Z-Boy rocker across from the sofa.

"Like I said, it wasn't a big deal," Lizbet said. "I didn't think either of you would be interested."

"You had a run-in with a bear!" The vein in Josie's neck looked ready to burst. "This never would have happened if you lived in East End!"

"I don't see how Lizbet's little incident has anything to do with where we live," Elizabeth said.

"Don't you? Really?" Josie sat down hard in an armless chair beside Elizabeth and pulled some brochures featuring grinning senior citizens involved in a host of outdoorsy activities out of her purse. After fanning them out on the table, Josie said, "Mom, I want you to consider these. Living out here in the backwoods is dangerous. You need to stop thinking only about yourself. Look at what happened to Lizbet!"

Elizabeth eyed Lizbet. "She looks right as rain to me. How are you feeling, sweet cheeks?"

"I'm totally fine," Lizbet said.

Josie groaned and pushed her hand through her severe haircut. "Where's Daugherty?"

"She's with my dad," Declan said.

"Does she have a phone with her? I bet she doesn't have a phone with her!" Josie huffed.

"Did you try calling her?" Lizbet asked.

Josie didn't answer but gave Lizbet the stink eye before turning back to Elizabeth. "Mother, this is no longer a safe place for you."

"Josie, this is my home. It's my whole world. I'm too old to create a new one." Elizabeth stood on wobbly legs. "You had something of an argument before Daugherty and Lizbet came, but now that they're here with me, you have to stop fussing."

"But Lizbet and the bear!"

"You make it sound like they're a comedy routine! And..." Elizabeth's voice faltered as curiosity got the better of her. "What really happened with the bear, dear?"

"We were helping with the search party for Courtney Derringer," Declan began.

"And I bumped into a bear," Lizbet finished for him. "Like I said, no big deal."

"A *bear*, Mother," Josie said.

"To be fair," Lizbet said, "I was walking in the woods. Sort of trespassing on his property."

"The bear doesn't get to have property!" Josie said.

And this is how we differ, Lizbet thought. "My point is, even if I had been living in town, I still might have encountered the bear if I had wanted to help with Courtney's search party. Meeting the bear had nothing to do with where we live."

Elizabeth looked pleased with Lizbet's answer. Josie much less so.

Declan leaned over and whispered in Lizbet's ear, "I want to go to Nicole's."

"What? Now?"

He nodded. "Your aunt gave me an idea."

Declan looked at his shoes as they walked to the barn. "I know it sounds weird, but I want to smell her room." He couldn't explain his newly heightened senses to Lizbet because it wasn't something he completely understood himself. "Besides, I can't think of a connection between Courtney and Jason other than Nicole."

"Poor Nicole. It must be devastating to lose a friend and your boyfriend in less than a week."

Declan tried to remember Courtney and Nicole ever being chummy, but he failed. "They played on the same team, but that doesn't mean they were friends."

"No?"

"I don't think they were. They're different. Courtney was more of a jock." He caught himself. "I mean, she is. Not she was."

Lizbet, as if sensing his sadness, looped her arm through his and began talking of the treatment she'd served Tickles to cure his wolfism. Declan only half-listened. The other half of him worried about the night, the full moon, and if anyone else would die.

Inside the barn, Lizbet retrieved the helmets, swung onto her bike, and turned the key in the ignition. Declan climbed on behind her and secured his helmet. Lizbet felt warm and solid as he slipped his arms around her waist and held tight. Somehow, she'd become his salvation. Without her, he wasn't sure he wanted to go on. Even with her, if he was in any way responsible for Jason's death or Courtney's disappearance, he wasn't sure he could live with himself.

They rumbled down the street, passing the quiet houses, disturbing a few restless dogs. As they drew closer to town, the yards grew smaller and the houses closer together. Lizbet turned down Nicole's street and cut the engine. Declan climbed off the bike, peeling away from her warmth.

"It doesn't look like they're home," Lizbet said.

Declan rocked back onto his heels. "That's right! They're gone! At the party, Nicole said her family was going boating on Lake Chelan."

"So she couldn't have had anything to do with Courtney's disappearance or Jason's death?"

"I guess not." He scratched his head. "I still want to smell her room."

She slid him a long glance. "You know how weird that sounds, right?"

"What can I say? My olfactory senses need satisfaction."

She nudged him. "Still weird..."

"Almost as weird as having a werewolf boyfriend?"

"That's weird, too," she said. "Do you think you can

satisfy your olfactory senses if we just stand under her window?" Lizbet's face tightened as she stared at the house.

He elbowed her. "Ready?"

"I don't know," she said, sounding young. "She might have a security alarm or a dog..."

"I'm sure you could win over the dog, if she had one—which she doesn't, by the way. I just want to smell her room."

"Right," Lizbet said, straightening her shoulders. "That shouldn't take long."

Declan nodded and stepped away from the sheltering hedge. His shoe landed on a twig, snapping it.

Somewhere down the street, a dog began to bark.

"Come on," Lizbet said, heading across the lawn.

Declan tried to follow her silently, but even his breathing sounded amplified. They dashed to the side of the house. Declan peeked in the first window, trying to remember the house's layout. "Dining room," he whispered. They jogged to the next window and found the kitchen. At the third window, the posters on the wall and the clothes strewn across the floor told him the room belonged to a teenage girl. He gasped when Nicole's smell wafted through the window, punching him in the gut.

"Why would the police mistake Nicole's jacket for Courtney's?" he asked. "Especially since Nicole isn't even in town."

"It was probably her parents who made the mistake, right? Nicole left her jacket..." Lizbet stopped herself. "Wait. The only thing telling us that coat belonged to Nicole

is your nose, and I know you have a lot of confidence in your olfactory senses, but..."

Declan had stopped listening as his gaze fastened on a pile of shredded rags poking out from the bottom of Nicole's closet. "I'm going in."

"Are you crazy?" Lizbet gasped.

He pointed at the strips of fabric lying on the floor. Leaning over Lizbet, he reached for the window sash.

"Wait!" Lizbet gripped his wrist. "You said yourself that there might be an alarm. Let me try it. You go and wait by the bike."

"So not happening. I didn't come here to watch you break into Nicole's room."

She reached past him and pulled on the sash. It opened easily.

They waited for several seconds, listening for a wailing alarm or a howling dog. When they heard nothing more startling than a call from a bird in the neighboring tree, Declan pulled the window all the way open and climbed inside. Lizbet followed.

Posters of rock stars lined the walls. Shelves holding a mishmash of novels, textbooks and framed photos of family and friends dominated one wall, while a large desk stacked with notebooks and papers took up another. A twinge of guilt hit him, but he reminded himself of the gurney and Jason's bloody body and the guilt died. The smell of the room, identical to the smell of the letterman jacket, engulfed Declan. He crossed the room in three long strides, dropped to his knees before the open closet and studied the torn rags on the floor.

He flashed back to his own shredded clothing. "She has to be a werewolf."

"That night in the woods when you were playing Sardines...is it possible she was bitten by Tickles?" Lizbet whispered.

"We probably don't have to whisper," Declan answered, his voice barely audible. "No one is here."

"Let's go," Lizbet said, her voice only slightly louder. "We saw what we came to see...and smell."

"I have to eat silver dust, raw hamburger, and sage?" Declan frowned at the silver dollar and hammer in his hands.

"Yep. It worked—maybe—for Tickles," Lizbet said. She stood at the kitchen table at Godwin's house, a package of raw hamburger on the counter in front of her. A wave of nausea washed through her as she unwrapped the meat. "But he's a little dog and you're not a small guy. I'm not sure it'll work." She crumbled up the sage and sprinkled it on top, filling the air with its sweet, tangy scent.

"What if it only partly works?"

"What do you mean?"

"Well, in my studies, I read about humans with dog heads."

"What? There's no such thing."

Declan's shoulders sagged. "If you can believe in werewolves, why not half-men and half-beasts? By the way, there's no half-man half-dog women—only men."

"I repeat, there's no such thing."

"You really need to be more open-minded," he told her, nodding at his books on the counter. "You can look it up for yourself." He took the silver dollar and hammer to the back porch. Seconds later, the sharp metallic sound of steel against silver filled the silence.

Lizbet flipped open a large book entitled *Mythical Beasts, Monsters, and Minotaur.*

> *The legends of dog-headed men (or according to Greek legend, cynoephali) are told all over the world. The Egyptian god Anubis, considered the god of death and the underworld, is perhaps the earliest recorded dog-headed creature. Paintings of him can be found throughout the Middle East.*
>
> *In the fifth century, a Greek doctor wrote about a tribe of dog-headed men who lived in India. Later, a Greek explorer described the dog-headed men as savages who communicated by barking.*
>
> *Marco Polo and Giovanni da Pian del Carpine both encountered barbaric dog-headed men during their travels in the Middle Ages.*
>
> *Centuries later, Saint Augustine made the argument*

that such men were not to be held to the same moral laws as mankind. Ancient icons of Saint Christopher show him with a dog head. Allegedly, he led a sinful life as a half-man half-beast. It wasn't until after his conversion and baptism that he transformed into a fully human man.

High in the Scottish mountains near Edinburgh, King Arthur supposedly battled an army of dog-headed soldiers. There are also reports of dog-headed men in fifth-century China and regions of Africa.

But not all records are ancient. There have been claims of sightings of humans with dog heads in the Himalayans, the Pacific Northwest, and the Shetland Islands.

Lizbet scanned the book for a more detailed account of the sighting in the Pacific Northwest. The word *Stehekin* caught her attention. An indescribable but powerful feeling swept through Lizbet. She set down the book.

Declan came into the room, carrying a handful of silver powder, and caught her expression.

"I want to go to Stehekin," she told him.

"What?" He poured the silver dust on top of the meat.

"Stehekin," she repeated. "It's based on a Salishan word meaning 'the way through.'" She cocked her head. "You've heard of it, right? It's at the northern tip of Lake Chelan and is the gateway to the Northern Cascade National Park."

"I don't really think I'm up for a road trip," Declan said. "The last thing I want to do is turn into a wolf while riding in a car with you."

"I can't really explain it, but I'm certain that Stehekin has answers."

Declan laid the hammer down on the table and met her gaze. "Lizbet, we don't even know the questions. How can we possibly find answers?"

"Even if this doesn't work, by tomorrow, you won't be a wolf for an entire month. We can go to Stehekin." She locked her eyes with his. "If you won't come with me, I'll have to go alone."

"Did you read about the dog-men?"

"It's ridiculous," she said, but even she heard the doubt in her voice.

"I have a theory."

She waited for him to continue.

"What if the dog-men are werewolves who were only half successful in finding a cure for wolfism?"

"Do you not want to try this?" she asked.

"I don't want to spend the rest of my life with a dog's head."

She wanted to laugh, but she knew from the look on Declan's face that he didn't think any of this was funny. A glance outside the window at the setting sun told her she'd need to leave soon. Using a wooden spoon, she mixed the silver dust into the hamburger.

"What do you think the sage is for?" Declan asked.

She lifted a shoulder. "To make it more palatable?"

"Hmm, not working," Declan said.

Lizbet dumped the concoction onto a paper plate and smiled at him. "Ready?"

He nodded.

"Are you sure you don't want me to stay?"

"I'm sure." After giving her a quick kiss, he took the plate from her and headed down the stairs. "See you tomorrow."

"I hope so," she whispered after he disappeared into the dark basement.

Rapscallion clambered out of the cupboard and greeted Lizbet with twitching whiskers.

She reached into her pocket and pulled out a crumble of cheese. "You know what to do," she said, offering the piece of Gouda to the mouse.

Chapter 6

Declan curled into a ball on the side of an unfamiliar hill. The hazy predawn light cast a grayish tint over the derelict cemetery. Dew and blades of grass clung to his bare skin. He sat up, self-conscious of his nudity. He could be arrested for this, although indecent exposure was a much lesser crime than murder. In his heart, he still found it hard to believe that he could have had anything to do with Jason's death or Courtney's disappearance, but he couldn't be sure.

He was unsure about almost everything now.

There was a time not too long ago when he'd thought he understood the world and how it worked. He'd loved science and despised anything that couldn't be explained.

He had become a thing he despised.

He pushed his hands through his hair, trying to remember last night's events and how he had gotten to this unfamiliar place. Glancing around, he took in the small clearing, the sad collection of weather-worn tombstones that leaned at odd angles like graying teeth in need of orthodontia. Moss and lichen clung to the stones like mold. Time had taken a toll on the lettering, rendering most of it indecipherable, but one name stood out, repeating itself from stone to stone: Stehekin.

Stehekin. It was a who as well as a where. The knowledge rocked through him, leaving him shivery and cold. He had to tell Lizbet. But how was he to get home when he didn't even know where he was? And what could he do for clothes?

Lizbet padded into the kitchen to find her mom stirring her bowl of cereal as if she were looking for something hidden among the bran flakes. Daugherty lifted her gaze to Lizbet and studied her.

"Something wrong?" Lizbet asked after saying good morning.

"Do you know where Declan is? John said he hasn't been home for several nights."

Lizbet blinked. "He's living with Gloria now."

"That's exactly what John thought." Daugherty went back to stirring her cereal. "But Gloria said he hasn't been sleeping there for the past few days. She thought he was at John's." Gloria lifted a spoonful of cereal and pointed it at Lizbet. "And now they both think he's been with you. Is there any reason for them to think that?"

"I've been here, with you, every night."

"And you don't know where Declan has been sleeping?"

Lizbet really hated lying to her mom—to anyone, really—but particularly to her mom. Besides, she understood why John and Gloria would be concerned. They should be. Especially if they knew the truth. She pulled a mug out of the cupboard and filled it with milk. "He hasn't been with me."

"And you don't know where he's been?"

Lizbet stirred chocolate into her milk before putting it into the microwave. Tired of dodging her mom's questions, she leaned against the counter. "He's been staying at Godwin's house."

"Godwin's? Why?" Daugherty set down her spoon.

"He wants to confront his stepfather."

"Good heavens, that's craziness!"

"Craziness. Yes, that's a good word for it." Lizbet longed to tell her mom of all the craziness, but she couldn't.

"He needs to let the police worry about Godwin." Daugherty cocked her head at Lizbet. "What's he thinking? You need to convince him he's being a loon."

Not a loon...a wolf, but she couldn't tell her mom that either.

Elizabeth shuffled into the room carrying a newspaper and shaking her head. "So sad." She put the paper down on the table and smoothed it out.

Daugherty let out a moan when she read the headline.

Lizbet pulled her cocoa from the microwave when it dinged before glancing over her mom and grandmother's

shoulders to read the paper's headline.

LOCAL BOY ESCAPES FROM JAIL. ONE DEPUTY DEAD IN CONFLICT

Malcolm Abbot, a suspect in the murder of Jason Norbit, escaped from his jail cell last night, leaving one deputy dead and another severely injured. The police are refusing to share clips from the security videos or photos of the condition of the cell, stating that the graphic images might incite undue alarm.

"Undue alarm? What could that mean?" Elizabeth wondered.

Lizbet and her mom exchanged glances, because Lizbet knew exactly what the police were trying to protect the public from.

Her phone buzzed and she took it and her cocoa outside to the back porch.

"Lizbet?"

"Declan, where are you?" she whispered.

"Harleson," he said. "I'm at a pay phone. I didn't even know they still had these."

"Where's Harleson?"

"Pretty much nowhere. Can you come and get me?"

"Sure." Pressing her phone between her ear and shoulder, she moved back into the kitchen and settled into the chair in front of the computer. She typed Harleson into the search engine. "It's seventy-five miles!"

"I know, but there's something here I have to show you. Can you come?"

Lizbet felt her mom's curious gaze on her back. "Yeah, but it will take me a while," she whispered as she slipped out the back door to avoid her mom's questions. If it would take her more than two hours to get there on her motorbike, she couldn't even imagine how long it would have taken Declan to get there on foot...or paws.

By the time Lizbet rolled into the one-street town, her legs were shaky and her fingers stiff. She'd bought the bike from Matias a few months ago. It was rusty-red with a cracked leather seat and worn-out tires, but she loved it—mostly because it gave her freedom to go wherever she pleased. But she'd never had to ride her bike so far before.

When she spotted Declan sitting on a street corner wearing a pair of what looked like mechanic's overalls, she burst out laughing despite her fatigue. She rolled up beside him, took off her helmet, and shook out her hair. "What are you wearing?"

He stood and pointed at the name embroidered in red lettering over his left breast. "Mike's overalls. I hope he doesn't want them back," he pulled the too-short and too-wide outfit away so he could peek down the zipper, "because I'm wearing nothing underneath."

"This could be a problem," Lizbet said. "Does Mike know you're wearing his suit?"

Declan shook his head. "We have to get out of here before he learns his truck was robbed. This looks like the sort of place where everyone knows each other and their wardrobes really well." He glanced up and down Main Street before putting his hand into the pocket and pulling out a handful of coins. "Thankfully for me, these were in the pocket, or else I never would have been able to call you.

Lizbet groaned. The thought of getting back on the bike depressed her. "Do you think they sell clothes anywhere?"

Declan motioned to the three taverns on the two blocks of Main Street. "I'm guessing they sell mostly beer. But I wouldn't know since I don't have a wallet and my call to you depleted my funds making my wardrobe a moot point."

"Let me get you some clothes and something to eat."

He nodded at the park across the street. "I'll hide out over there in case Mike comes looking for his duds."

Lizbet pulled open the glass doors of Donna's One Stop Shop. A large woman with arms the size of Lizbet's thighs sat at the counter reading a magazine. She glanced up when a jingling bell announced Lizbet's arrival.

"Anything I can help you find, darlin'?"

Lizbet glanced around the crowded store. A clothes rack lined the back wall. A refrigerator case ran along the side. The store was so small Lizbet felt sure she'd find

everything she never wanted in minutes. "I'd rather look on my own, thanks," she told the woman.

"Suit yourself," the woman said, and she bent back over her magazine.

Lizbet rifled through the clothes rack and tried to sort her thoughts. What had Declan been so anxious for her to see? Curiosity and impatience hurried her.

A few minutes later, Lizbet left Donna's with a brown paper bag carrying some donuts, apples, a liter of orange juice, a pair of running shorts, a T-shirt that read *I love unicorns* and a pair of red, white, and blue flip-flops.

Declan peeked in the bag. "Unicorns? Really?"

"It was better than the other options."

He cocked an eyebrow.

"You'll just have to trust me."

He rolled his eyes and disappeared into a public restroom. Moments later, he emerged wearing the clothes. "I feel ridiculous."

"But at least no one will mistake you for Mike and ask you to fix their muffler."

"There's that."

"What did you want to show me?"

He motioned to her bike. "You okay if I drive?"

"That would be good." And she handed him the key.

The cemetery was about a mile from town on a dirt road that led to an abandoned barn. Declan knew this because he'd first taken the road to the dead end before turning around. He felt lucky that he'd found Harleson and not followed the road into the thick of the Cascade Mountains.

He rolled the bike up to the stone wall surrounding the gravestones and pointed. "Stehekin is not only a place—it's a family name."

Lizbet got off the bike and headed for the tombstones like a person magnetized. She dropped to her knees and used the end of her shirt to wipe one marker clean.

> *Malki our brother, kind and mild,*
> *Was loved by folks and the wild,*
> *The moon, stars, and sun loved him best*
> *Malki spoke to the wind, both east and west.*

"I wonder what it means?" Declan asked as he opened the brown bag from Donna's and pulled out the donut.

Lizbet didn't answer, but got to her feet and went to another marker with an inscription.

> *Helda spoke to all loving beings*
> *Trees, plants, flowers and things*
> *And creatures conversed in kind,*
> *Wind, sun, rocks and mind.*

"Can these people be your family?" Declan asked right before polishing off the last bit of donut. He wiped his sticky fingers on the dew-damp grass.

"Do you think they're Ollos Verdes?"

"The who?"

"Didn't I tell you about that legend?" Lizbet asked. "Matias and Maria's mawmaw told it to me."

"You may have, but remind me."

Lizbet tried to remember everything Mawmaw had told her about the Ollos Verdes. "A long time ago, the world was made of two equal parts. Animals lived in the water and people lived in a sky full of fertile fields, soaring mountains, and flower-filled valleys. One day, a Sky Child grew weary and fell asleep beneath the spreading branches of an apple tree. She slipped down a hole. Frightened, she wrapped her arms around the tree and it too fell through the sky.

"She called for help and fortunately for her, two swans were swimming in the water-world below. They rose to save her. Spreading their wings, they formed a soft nest for the girl to lie upon. 'What can I do now?' the girl asked. 'Can you return me to the sky world?'

"But the birds were frightened to fly so close to the sun. 'We'll take you to Big Turtle,' said one swan. 'He knows everything,' said the other.

"Big Turtle listened to the girl's story of a world with fertile land, tall mountains, and flower-filled fields.

"'If we can get some soil, we can create our own earth of land, sky, and water,' Big Turtle said.

"'But where can we find the soil?' Swan asked.

"''Tis below the water,' Big Turtle told them. 'We must dig deep.'

"Otter, Beaver, and Muskrat argued over who would go.

"'I'm the fastest,' said Otter.

"'But I'm the strongest,' said Beaver.

"'But I can swim the farthest,' said Muskrat.

"A little toad popped out of the water. 'I'll go. I can dive very deep.'

"The other animals laughed and mocked.

"'You're too small,' said Beaver.

"'You're too ugly,' said Otter.

"'You're too slow,' said Muskrat.

"'Hush!' Big Turtle said in a loud voice. 'We are all equal, and we're all able to do our best. We will need the efforts of all.'

"The vain Otter smoothed his glossy fur, took a deep breath, and disappeared into the water. Beaver slapped his tail against the water before diving in. Muskrat followed. One by one they returned, gasping for air.

"'It's too deep,' said Otter.

"'It's too dark,' said Beaver.

"'No one can dive so deep,' said Muskrat.

"'I will go,' said Toad, before she sucked in a deep breath and disappeared beneath a wave.

"'We will never see her again,' said Otter.

"'She will die from bravery,' said Beaver.

"'She will surely drown,' said Muskrat.

"Moments later, Swan pointed at bubbles breaking the water's surface. Toad's ugly face appeared. She spat a

mouthful of soil onto Big Turtle's back before sinking to the bottom of the sea.

"Big Turtle commanded all the creatures to rub the soil into his shell. The seeds of grain sprouted and grew and grew until a large island was formed. It grew into the world as we know it today.

"Eventually, the sky people noticed and grew envious. More and more fell from the hole in the sky to join our world. But only the descendants of the first Sky Child are the Earth's people. They are the Ollos Verdes—the green-eyed ones. Only they can converse with the Earth and its creations."

"I bet you're one of the Ollos Verdes," Declan said.

"I don't know," she said slowly. "I wonder how I knew the answer had something to do with Stehekin."

Declan sat down on the stone wall and watched the entranced Lizbet move around the cemetery. "I've been thinking about that. Have you ever heard of genetic memory?"

She shook her head without looking at him and kept her gaze on the tombstones. She touched them with reverence and studied them as if they had something more to tell her than names and dates.

"It's the theory that we inherit memories, talents, and skills in our DNA from our ancestors."

She tore her attention away from the tombstones to shoot him a quick glance. "That doesn't sound like something you would believe in."

"Recently, I believe in a lot of things I didn't used to. It's amazing how a little thing like becoming a werewolf can make you open-minded."

She turned to him. "You didn't kill Jason Norbit."

Declan swallowed hard and studied his hands. He wanted to believe that so badly, but he couldn't. Not without some sort of proof.

"Did you know Malcolm Abbot?" Lizbet asked.

"I know Malcolm. Quiet kid. Small. Played on the chess team."

"Did you know he was arrested for Jason's murder?"

Declan shook his head, listening in disbelief while Lizbet told him what she'd read in the paper.

"You couldn't have had anything to do with his escape because you were here."

He opened his mouth to argue.

She cut him off. "If you were on the security video, the police would be looking for you."

"Not if I looked like a wolf."

She sat down close enough for their thighs to touch. "You were here—or were on your way here. You couldn't have had anything to do with Malcolm's escape or the deputy's death."

He hung his head, still feeling helpless and hopeless.

"It's disappointing the meat concoction didn't work," Lizbet said.

"We don't know whether I ate it or not," Declan said.

"Yes, we do."

"The mouse?" he guessed.

Lizbet nodded.

Declan put his hand over the unicorn on his belly. "I really ate raw hamburger?"

"And silver dust."

Declan felt ill, and it didn't have anything to do with the dry donut he'd just eaten.

Lizbet bounced to her feet and went to kneel beside a stone partially covered by ivy and tall grass. She brushed the plants away to read the inscription to him.

> *"Winds that blow sweeter songs,*
> *Carry seeds and right the wrongs."*

A chill passed over Declan as a cold wind picked up and tossed leaves and twigs into the air.

"Lizbet."

"What?" She remained in front of the tombstone, pulling the ivy vines away and breaking off the shoots of grass.

She hadn't noticed.

"The wind. You called the wind."

She twisted around to smile at him. "Don't be silly."

Declan held up his hand to test the breeze. "I'm not being silly. Two seconds ago, the air was hot and still. You read that, and now there's wind." He strode to the closest grave, wishing it could speak in more than rhymes.

Lizbet pushed back her hair and frowned at him. "I can communicate with animals. It's not that remarkable.

People everywhere do. The difference is, I stop to listen to what they have to say."

Declan knelt beside her and took her face in his hands. "You don't think it's remarkable because you're used to it. I'm telling you, I don't know anyone else—other than Dr. Doolittle, who was fictional, by the way—who can do what you do. So, yes, you're remarkable."

She pulled away and fell onto her butt. "I think everyone is capable of communicating with animals. It's just most people don't take the time to learn their language because they don't think it's even a possibility. Growing up in isolation like I did forced me to reach out to them."

"No. That's not it. You are amazing." He nodded at the tombstone. "Try the rain one."

"Why?"

"I want to see if you can summon the rain. Imagine all the good you could do if you could make it rain in countries suffering from droughts."

She shook her head. "I wouldn't want that kind of power."

"Why not? Think of the people dependent on agricultural—"

"What if I make it rain, but then I can't make it stop? What if—"

He cut her off. "Just try it."

"I'm afraid."

"See? This is exactly why you have the ability."

"I don't have special abilities."

"Yes, you do. And the reason you have them is because they humble you. Someone else might be motivated to use them for greed or gain or vengeance. But not you. You're so good you—"

She placed her fingers on his lips. "Stop it. I'm not who you think I am."

He grabbed her wrist. "You don't even know how amazing you are." They stared at each other. "Just read that." He nodded at the tombstone.

"If I read it, will you stop this? Can we go?" She glanced up at the clouds gathering on the horizon. The wind tugged at her curls. "We need to leave. Riding in the rain is miserable."

"Sure. We'll go as soon as you read that." He pulled the ivy away from the grave and ripped out the tall blades of grass in the way. He'd promised they'd leave as soon as she'd summoned the rain, but now that he knew there was a stanza about lightning, he really wanted her to do that one, too.

She sighed before she started.

> *"Weeping rain to cleanse the earth,*
> *Bring us life, a new rebirth."*

A few raindrops fell.

She stood and brushed off her jeans. "This means nothing. The rainclouds have been gathering all morning."

"And they just happened to fall after you read the tombstone!" He held out his hand. "Give me your phone."

"What for?"

"We need to take a picture of this. It could come in handy."

She pulled her phone out of her pocket and handed it to him. "I'm going along with this not because I think I had anything to do with the weather, but because I want to capture these names. Maybe I can look them up on some sort of genealogical site."

He grinned. "Good plan." He took a quick photo of all the gravesites before returning the phone to Lizbet. Hope, something that had disappeared the moment he learned he was a werewolf, started to seep back in. If Lizbet could control the weather, maybe he could control being a werewolf. Maybe his future wasn't as bleak as he thought.

Chapter 7

The next morning, Gloria set down her coffee mug and studied her son. "Declan, we need to talk."

Declan glanced outside at the midmorning sun. The moon had passed. He'd slept through the night in his own bed. It was going to be a good day. Even if he did hate days that began with "we need to talk." Because conversations that began with "we need to talk" were typically to be avoided.

"As you know, your dad and I don't always see eye-to-eye on everything, but right now, we agree on this."

Great. He hated it when his parents colluded. Declan poured himself a cup of coffee, but kept his back to his mom so she wouldn't see him if he decided he needed an eye-roll.

"Your recent behavior is scaring me. You've disappeared for nights on end."

Declan set his mug on the table before helping himself to a bowl of Captain Crunchies.

"Now, I understand that if you'd been able to follow your original plan, you would have been leaving for Duke and living on your own. And honestly, I think I would have preferred that to your unhealthy obsession with Lizbet."

"I haven't been staying with Lizbet."

"That's what your dad said, because I guess that's what her mom told him."

Declan poised his spoon above his cereal bowl. "What do you mean you 'guess that's what her mom told him'?"

"Well, she could be covering for Lizbet…"

Declan hunched his shoulders and returned to eating his cereal. "You think her mom is lying? For me?"

"And her daughter." Gloria swallowed her coffee before returning her mug to the table. "But frankly, as much as I hate the idea of you and Lizbet setting up house together, I find the other explanation—the one John gave me—twice as abhorrent."

"And that is?"

"You're staying at Godwin's house? How could you be so stupid? You know he's dangerous."

Declan thought about pointing out that his mom had been the one to marry him.

"That behavior stopped yesterday! I changed the locks." She peered at him over the rim of her coffee mug. "But I suspect you already know that, seeing as how you stayed the night here."

Declan pushed away his cereal bowl. "Mom, do you want to put a tracking device on me?"

"No! You know I love having you here." She covered his hand with her left hand. "If I'm honest, I'm mad at myself about that."

"Mom..."

"I am. You don't need to stay here. I'm coping fine."

"You know my being here isn't just about you, right?" Declan lied. Since the accident that had nearly severed her right hand, his mom had been forced to learn how to be left-handed. This meant that she had most of her purchases, including groceries and meals, delivered. Still, because she found feeding herself awkward, she'd lost a lot of weight. She rarely bathed, showered, or left the house. In a more introverted person, this probably would have been okay, but for his A-personality mom, this hermit lifestyle was skirting the edges of scary. "There's also the winery."

Gloria blew out a breath. "We should sell that."

Declan shook his head, thinking about Matias's mawmaw's amazing wine. If he could somehow get a hold of that recipe... The blackberry wine from his grandfather's winery was close, but it lacked the magic. If only he could bottle the magic...

"I thought you wanted to be a doctor," his mom said.

"I do."

"You have school—you don't have time to run a business."

He slid her glance. "Should I ask Holbrook St. James to hire someone to oversee it?"

She flushed a pretty pink and hid her face behind her coffee mug. "That's a good plan."

He twisted his hand beneath hers so he could entwine their fingers. "I love you, Mom."

She blinked back tears. "I love you, too. I just don't want to see you throwing away your future."

"Lizbet is my future."

"Maybe, but maybe not. And even if she is a part of it, she can't be your entire life."

"She's won't be. She has her own life, too."

"Like what?"

"Well, today she's working."

"And what are you going to do?"

Other than rejoice he wasn't a werewolf? Other than give thanks that the remedy hadn't turned him into a dog-headed man? A thought came to him. "I'm going to go and play chess in Seattle."

"Chess?" Gloria rocked back in her chair.

"Yeah. At those giant chessboards in Westlake Park."

"I didn't know you like chess!"

He didn't, but Malcolm did and if Declan wanted to find Malcolm, he needed to look where he thought Malcolm might hide.

"Westlake Park. Isn't it pretty rough down there?"

"There's a lot of homeless people, if that's what you mean." Declan poured himself another bowl of cereal. "Supposedly, a lot of the homeless are chess whizzes." Declan thought about asking his mom what she intended to do that day but since after her accident she'd taken to

spending each day in front of the TV with a crossword puzzle book, he decided not to bring it up.

"Are you going alone?"

"Why? Do you want to come?"

Gloria glanced at the clock on the microwave. "No. Actually, Holbrook St. James will be here in a couple of hours." She twisted her lips. "It'll take me that long to shower and do my hair."

He grinned. "I'm sure you can go over your taxes without doing your hair."

"We're not doing taxes."

"Ha." He pushed his cereal around his bowl. "So, is this like a date?"

She shook her head. "I'm not sure what it is." An embarrassed and shy expression, a look he wasn't used to seeing on his mom's face, settled in as she bit her lip. "I have a really bad track record when it comes to men." She caught herself and lifted her mug at him. "Although, your dad is a good guy."

Declan didn't want a conversation where his mom once again defended her choice of leaving his dad for Godwin. Godwin had turned out to be a monster. Literally. And then, almost immediately following his disappearance, she'd had a brief fling with her attorney, Leo Cabriolet, who had also disappeared—because he'd been a werewolf captured by Lizbet and killed by a bear. Although his mom only knew that Cabriolet had disappeared. Declan hoped to keep it that way. "I like St. James."

"He's kind of a nerd."

Declan winked at her. "I like nerds."

Gloria shook her head. "You like weirdos."

"Mom, she's not a weirdo."

"Well, she's definitely a free spirit."

Declan smiled. "That's what I like about her."

Because Mr. Neal liked to play classical music to his plants, Lizbet had gotten so she could hum along to Mozart's *Eine kleine Nachtmusik* and Bach's fugues. She really hated Wagner, and she suspected that the plants did, too. They always looked a little droopy and yellow after one of Wagner's operas. Or maybe she was just projecting her feelings onto the plants. But on this morning, Nicole Gunner interrupted Beethoven's *Ode to Joy,* and because Lizbet minded, she kept her hose trained on the vegetable shelves.

She knew Nicole partly blamed her for Declan's decision to ditch his plans to attend Duke and stay local, but Lizbet also knew that Declan would have dropped out of school before he would have left his mom after her accident. If Nicole knew Declan as well as she thought she did, she would know that, too. Still, Lizbet had to concede that it must hurt to have Declan change his mind, leaving her going to Duke alone and friendless.

Nicole brushed her long blond hair off her shoulder and sent Lizbet a phony smile as she crossed the sawdust-strewn nursery floor.

"Can I help you find something?" Lizbet asked.

Nicole placed her hands on her hips. She had a figure like a long blade of grass. Her golden hair added to the image. If Nicole had been shorter, she'd be hard to find in a wheat field. She had pinky-white skin and delicate features. "I think you know who I'm looking for."

Lizbet turned off her hose and it dribbled at her side. "Declan quit working here after his grandfather died."

"Oh, I know that."

"Then why did you think he'd be here?"

"Because you are." Nicole sniffed as if she found something odiferous.

Lizbet glanced at the bags of fertilizer lining the back wall. She didn't mind the smell, but she knew most people did.

"I'm not the only one looking for him. There's an entire pack." Nicole paused, letting her words sink in.

"I'm not Declan's keeper."

"Oh, I know that." Nicole fingered the silver necklace at her throat. Didn't there used to be a cross at the end of that chain? And why would Nicole use the word 'pack'? Was it Lizbet's imagination, or had Nicole emphasized the word?

"Then why are you here? I don't know where Declan is right now."

"Maybe right now you don't, but you will. I need you

to tell him something from me."

Lizbet turned her hose back on. Her fingers itched to spray Nicole. "Why don't you just tell him yourself? It's not like he's hard to find."

"But he has been. Where was he all day yesterday?"

"Why?" Lizbet didn't mean to raise her voice, but she must have because Mr. Neal poked his head out of his office.

"Lizbet, is there a problem?" His gaze ran over Nicole and a flicker of a frown crossed his expression.

"No problem, Mr. Neal. I just can't help Nicole find what she's looking for."

"Oh." Mr. Neal emerged from behind the door and smoothed down his apron. "Is there something in particular you need? We can always special order it."

"It's a who, not an it," Nicole said.

This was probably not the wisest thing to say to Mr. Neal, who considered his plants just as important as people—if not more so. He believed that humans, who could defend themselves physically and emotionally, should protect creatures—including plants—who could not. He could talk for hours about the human condition and the sacred roles people possessed, but rarely assumed, as caretakers of the earth and its creations.

"She's looking for Declan," Lizbet told him.

The frown hovering behind Mr. Neal's eyes came out of hiding. He clearly considered Declan Lizbet's concern, not Nicole's. "Declan left my employ several weeks ago."

"Oh, I know," Nicole said.

Mr. Neal, a mild-mannered, gentle man, bristled, reminding Lizbet of a Venus flytrap ready to snap. "Then I'm not sure why you think we can help you."

"I just wanted to pass along a message." Nicole narrowed her eyes at Lizbet. "Tell him no one likes a lone wolf." After that, she turned on her heel and strode away.

"What was that supposed to mean?" Mr. Neal blinked at Lizbet before shaking his head. "What an unpleasant girl."

Lizbet didn't agree. Mostly because if she had to guess, she'd say that Nicole was no longer a girl. She'd turned into a wolf.

Chapter 8

Skyscrapers and clouds shaded Westlake Park in the center of downtown Seattle. A light breeze toyed with the fur of a standard poodle standing sentinel beside his master at a chess table. Businessmen's ties bounced as they paced across the park on their lunch hour. A group of homeless people and businessmen gathered around a large chessboard painted on the cement with knee-high pawns, but more than one game was going on. Several small tables were set up throughout the park with players frowning in concentration as they sat contemplating their moves and spectators watched in reverent silence. It was both a stupid and brilliant place to hide. What was the best hiding place? A city to meld into? Or a wilderness where no one ever goes?

Declan's gaze shifted from the weather-beaten faces of the homeless to the smooth shaven chins of the business set as he searched for Malcolm. Of course, he didn't really expect to find him. Why would he be able to do what the police couldn't? But, as far as he knew, the police didn't have his heightened sense of smell.

Not that he was exactly sure what Malcolm smelled like. After all, they hadn't known each other all that well, despite the fact that they'd gone to school together since kindergarten.

Malcolm was small and not at all athletic. He didn't hang out in the locker room or on the basketball court unless he had to. But he had been captain of the chess team, which was why Declan had decided to look for him at Westlake Park. He'd gone by Malcolm's house earlier, hoping to catch a whiff of his scent. But the stench of fear overrode everything else on that street.

Declan was only beginning to understand emotions and how they could cloud and permeate every situation. Including a manhunt. Fear stank like urine with the same pungent repulsion, only worse. Many of the people gathered in the park reeked of marijuana, but there were other smells—a few that he was only beginning to recognize. The businessmen carried secrets, which had their own tang, as did a few of the housewives. The mothers with babies in strollers had their own pressing worries and concerns. Their fears were sweeter than the stench he'd found at Malcolm's parents' home.

A sudden movement caught his eye. A goth girl hunkered at a table and pulled her black hoodie to shield

her face. Her hand hovered over a bishop on the board. Her fingers were blunt, thick, too thick for a girl her size. She wore a gypsy-style skirt and a loose lacy blouse beneath her black hoodie. Courtney?

No. Malcolm.

Declan strode across the park and dropped to a squat beside the table. "Check," he said.

"It ain't over till it's over," the man in dirty battle fatigues opposite Malcolm said.

"It's not at all over," Declan said. He pointed out a move for the man to make.

The man used his queen as Declan suggested and declared, "Checkmate!" He bounced from his chair to do a victory dance.

"What are you doing?" Malcolm asked.

"Ending this game," Declan said as he slipped into the seat the dancing man had vacated.

"I'd try to run, but it'd be pretty pointless even if I wasn't wearing these stupid heels." Malcolm frowned as he lined the chess pieces back along the edges of the board. "Are you going to turn me in?"

"Do you want me to?"

Malcolm shrugged. "I don't know. This isn't much of an existence. My whole life has been smashed to hell."

"Your parents are scared."

"They should be. I'm scared, too." Malcolm's hands shook as he moved his pawns. "I didn't mean to hurt anyone."

"What happened?"

"You wouldn't believe me if I told you."

"I probably would."

"No. No way." Malcolm's shoulder also started twitching and Declan wondered if he was on the verge of tears.

Declan looked around, wondering if anyone could overhear them, but then decided it didn't matter. No one would believe him if they could. "I'm a werewolf."

Malcolm stopped fussing with the chess pieces and stared at Declan with his coal-rimmed eyes.

"So I can believe almost anything," Declan continued.

Malcolm leaned forward, his elbows on the table. "What do you know?"

"I'm not sure what you mean, but I know on the mornings after a full moon, I wake up outside, naked, sometimes bloodstained, without any memory of what happened during the night."

Malcolm nodded. "It was like that for me, too, at first."

"What changed?"

Malcolm's gaze lingered on the group of yogis across the park balancing on one leg with their hands pressed together in front of their chests as if in prayer. "It'll sound bizarre, but I really worked on becoming more self-aware."

"Self-aware?"

He slowly nodded. "It's a head game. Takes a lot of concentration, especially when I'm a wolf and all I can think about is finding something—anything—to eat. But yeah, I've gotten so I can remember most nights. Even when the moon is full. Even at midnight, when I think I'm totally losing it. That's how I know I didn't kill that deputy."

Declan rocked back, surprised. "Do you know who did?"

Malcolm lifted a shoulder. "Pack members."

"Other wolves?"

"They killed Jason, too."

Declan took a moment to let this information sweep through him. Relief, more powerful than a drug, surged. "Are you sure?" he asked in a strangled voice.

"Yeah. Jason was a," he made air quotes around the words, "traitorous pack member." Jason swallowed hard. "And they made it clear the same thing would happen to me if I crossed them."

"I guess I'm lucky I haven't met them."

It was Malcolm's turn to look surprised. "The pack hasn't reached out to you?"

"No. I don't know anything about a pack." Which wasn't completely true, since he'd seen Leo Cabriolet as a werewolf.

Malcolm reached into his hood to scratch his greasy black hair. "That's weird."

"It's all weird."

Malcolm quirked an eyebrow.

"What are you going to do?" Declan dropped his voice to a whisper. "The police think you're responsible for killing that deputy and Jason."

"I have to find out who did it." He frowned. "That's why the pack hates me. They want me to join them, and

all I want is my life back. I don't want to hang out with a bunch of dogs in some house in the woods."

"Leo Cabriolet didn't live with dogs in the woods."

Malcolm glanced over his shoulder, stood, and motioned for Declan to follow him. "You never know who's listening," he said under his breath as he tottered on his high heels. "You've got to be careful. It's impossible to tell who is who."

"There can't be that many werewolves," Declan whispered.

"There's more than werewolves."

"What?" Declan forgot to whisper.

"You thought werewolves were the only monsters?" He shook his head as if Declan were an especially stupid student. "No. There are witches, wizards, ghosts, vampires, valkyries."

Declan glanced around at the briefcase-carrying businesspeople, the moms pushing baby strollers, the teens on skateboards, and the rough and tired-looking homeless.

"It's impossible to tell them apart from anyone else," Malcolm said.

"Then how did you learn about them?"

"Well, for one thing, members of the pack introduced themselves the day after I first turned. Then they broke me out jail. That was a nightmare...I can't believe..." His voice trailed away as he thought. "Why would they reach out to me and not you?"

"Wait." A thought occurred to Declan. "Who's the alpha?"

"A huge black wolf. I've never seen him in human form."

"It's got to be Godwin."

"Who?"

"My stepfather. He hates me. Tried to kill me."

"Then it can't be him," Malcolm said.

"Why not?"

"Because if the alpha wanted to kill you, you'd be dead already."

On her way home from work, Lizbet made two stops. The first at a grocery store for a bag of unshelled raw peanuts. The second in the woods bordering the park behind Nicole's house.

Lizbet parked her motorbike against a tree, pulled the helmet off her head, and grabbed the bag of nuts from her backpack. Children ran around the park and climbed up the jungle gym. Mothers and nannies pushed toddlers on the swings. Some boys played soccer in the field while a girl and her dad tried to coax a kite into a windless sky. Lizbet watched the girl and her father for a few minutes. After a moment, she quietly whispered,

> *"Gentle breeze, hear my plea,*
> *Leave thy corners and come to me."*

A soft wind replied. The kite swelled and lifted. Lizbet whispered, "Thank you."

She didn't know what it meant or what she could do with this newfound power. It humbled and frightened her. She didn't think anyone, let alone herself, should possess such a gift. But then, if she did, shouldn't she learn how to use it? Wisely? It should be about more than making kites fly and keeping parties from being rained out. Where had that spell come from? Had she thought it up at just that moment? Or was it something she'd learned long ago and nearly forgotten?

For one of the first times—that she knew of—she longed for her real mom. Of course, she considered Daugherty her real mom. She couldn't imagine loving anyone more than she loved Daugherty, but she missed Rose—the mom she could barely remember—because she was sure Rose had things to teach her that Daugherty never could.

She tried to recall Rose and pulled up flashes of memory. Cuddling in front of flames roaring in the fireplace. Fishing along the banks of the gentle stream near the cottage. Pulling weeds from the garden. Collecting fat, squiggly worms for their fishing hooks. Gathering eggs from the chickens and spreading seeds...

"What are you doing with those nuts?" a squirrel in a nearby tree chattered at her.

Lizbet startled out of her memories. "They're for you," she said with a smile.

"Why?" Squirrels were stingy—hoarders by nature—and therefore suspicious of generosity.

Lizbet glanced around to make sure no one was watching

or listening. An old man with a metal detector moved closer to her, swinging his machine, so she motioned for the squirrel to follow as she stepped deeper into the woods. Above her, the squirrel darted through the branches, following.

"I want to know if the girl in the yellow house behind the hedge is a werewolf," Lizbet said once she was sure she couldn't be overheard by the man with his noisy toy.

"She is," the squirrel said.

"Are you sure?"

"I can prove it," the squirrel told her. He waved a tiny paw at her before scampering through the forest.

Lizbet had to jog to keep up.

The squirrel scurried down the tree and darted beneath fern fronds. *"See? She sheds her fur when the moon is full."*

Lizbet knelt, pushed the ferns aside and saw a pile of shredded pink material. A few feet farther lay what remained of a pair of jeans. She nodded, satisfied. "This is a big bag of nuts for one squirrel."

"Oh, I'll share," the squirrel lied.

Lizbet nodded again, as if she believed him. Which she didn't.

"There's this place where all the paranormals hang," Malcolm told Declan as they walked along a busy Seattle sidewalk. "It's like a bar, but instead of carding you, they've got these giant trolls guarding the door."

"Trolls?"

"You would think they were bodybuilders." Malcolm slid him a glance. "You didn't think normal people were really built like that, did you?"

"Wait, you're telling me all muscular people are trolls?" He shook his head. "Sorry, don't believe it. Baxter..."

"Dresden definitely has troll blood in his ancestry."

Declan scratched his head. "Would they let him in, even if he's just a fraction of a troll?"

Malcolm nodded. "It's pretty inclusive. There's only one rule, but people seem to have a hard time following it. The trolls will take you out if you break it."

"What's that?"

"No fighting. But like I said, the paranormals struggle with it."

"By 'take you out,' what do you mean? They kick you out?"

"If you're lucky, that's all. The trolls have a really low tolerance level. Make them mad, and you're dead."

Declan swallowed and watched the people moving past him. Suddenly, no one seemed normal. Anyone could be a vampire, a witch, a valkyrie... and he wasn't even sure what that was. A man in a kilt. A woman with an afro. A guy with an unlit reefer between his teeth. "Take me there?"

"I'm not sure they'll let you in."

"Why not? I wasn't lying about being a wolf."

"I know. I can smell you."

"That's gross."

"But true."

"Yeah, I guess." He realized he should have known Malcolm was a werewolf just by his scent. "So why wouldn't they let me in?"

"If the alpha hates you, you'd be shunned, if not killed. Pack members are not allowed to kill each other unless the alpha decides you're a threat to the pack." He paused. "I'm surprised you're still alive."

"Does the alpha go there?"

"He has a private entrance. He usually doesn't mingle with the riffraff."

"Sounds like a peach."

"The most dangerous piece of fruit I know."

"So you know him."

"We've met, yes." Malcolm came to a stop in front of a glistening glass-and-chrome building on the water's edge. Limousines were parked in a circular drive. Hulking doormen guarded the wide entrance. A marble statue of a winged angel carrying a spear floated above a burbling fountain as if suspended midair. Silver swirls painted the words *Wonderlust, members only* on the glass wall.

"I owe him...and the pack. They're the ones who sprang me from that jail cell. Just talking to you is probably a serious mistake. As a member of the pack, it's a given that I hate anyone the alpha hates." He turned away, his shoulders sagging. "But I don't want to be a part of the pack." His words sounded like a whispered prayer. "I just want my life back."

"What can I do to help?" Declan asked.

"I'm not sure you can." Malcolm swallowed. "But I know someone who might be able to."

"I'm not sure how you think your girlfriend is going to help," Malcolm said later that night as they sat at a café near the waterfront. The late summer sun hung at the edge of the horizon, moments away from setting. It wouldn't be dark until almost ten and according to Malcolm, the Wonderlust wouldn't pick up steam until close to midnight. "If she's not a paranormal, she'll just get in the way."

Declan didn't feel comfortable sharing Lizbet's secrets, but he did know that he felt safer around Lizbet than anyone else. "Consider it like a double date."

"Courtney doesn't think of me that way," Malcolm said, but his tone of voice said that he wished she would. "Listen, I know you're new to all this, but you should know that in the paranormal world, there's a hierarchy and some pretty established rivalries."

"Yeah?"

Malcolm nodded and picked up his hamburger. "So, for example, werewolves and vampires hate each other. Shape shifters who can transform into anything they want pretty much despise mere werewolves. Welcome to the bottom rung of the supernatural world."

"Thanks," Declan said.

"And, I hate to be the one to break this to you, but as a turned creature, you are the lowliest of the low."

Declan stirred a French fry in a squirt of ketchup. "What do you mean, *turned creature*?"

"There are two ways to become a werewolf. You can be born one, or you can be turned. You were turned. Those who are born and raised are considered a step above those who are turned." Declan's thoughts went back to the night Lizbet and the animals confronted the wolves. He'd been bitten on the hand by the wolf Leo Cabriolet, his mom's attorney by day and werewolf by night. He hadn't thought much of it at the time. His mind had been twisted by so many things: Lizbet conversing with animals, wolves shifting into humans, bears lumbering away with naked attorneys...all of it so overwhelming and totally unbelievable. And now this...

"Interesting." Declan munched on a French fry. "And how do the paranormals feel about creatures like you and me who don't want to be werewolves?"

"They don't understand it. After all, there are a lot of benefits. You don't age. You heal incredibly fast. You have amazing strength. Heightened senses. And sexually—"

Declan stopped him. "And you want to be turned back why?"

Malcolm put down his hamburger. "This is not the life I had in mind, you know? I wanted...no, I want to be a scientist. Being a werewolf messes with my head."

"I get that." Declan stared at the ketchup on his plate. It looked like blood and made him sick. He didn't want to inhale his hamburger, but even when he wasn't a wolf he still had a raging appetite.

Malcolm toyed with his French fries. "Nothing makes sense anymore."

"So, if you could snap your fingers, you'd go back before you were turned?"

Malcolm started to nod, but then stopped. "At first, I thought so, but now I'm not exactly sure."

Declan followed his gaze. Courtney Derringer, dressed in a stunning blue dress that showed off her long, strong legs, climbed out of a Mascrati idling at the Wonderlust's curb. She flipped her reddish hair over her shoulder, greeted the troll guards and sashayed through the doors. Declan had never considered Courtney as hot, but tonight she smoldered. He wondered how much she factored into Malcolm's indecision.

"How have they not found her?"

"Witches can be hard to pin down."

"The Puritans did it."

"Those witches were posers."

"Are you sure about that?" Declan asked.

"A witch isn't caught unless she wants to be."

Lizbet followed Declan's directions to the water's edge. The moon sat on the horizon, casting a long shimmery beam of light that led to a glistening chrome and glass building. He waved at her from a café across the street. Putting the motorbike in gear, she wedged it into a parking space.

He greeted her with a kiss and introduced her to Malcolm. "Here, I got you something."

She peeked into the shopping bag from an elite store. "What's this?"

"A dress, shoes, and jewelry."

The silky green fabric would match her eyes. The silver curled around emerald stones on the pendant looked real. Confused, she didn't know what to say, other than, "Declan?"

He nodded at the club across the street where limousines clustered around the entrance like ducks waiting for crumbs at a pond. "We're going in there and we want to fit in."

She glanced at his jeans and T-shirt and he read her doubts. "I bought new duds for me, too."

She cocked an eyebrow. "We're underage," she reminded him.

"It won't matter in there."

"To who?"

"They won't turn us away," Declan said.

Malcolm cleared his throat. "She's mortal."

"She's more powerful than both of us," Declan told him.

Malcolm looked skeptical.

"Trust me," Declan said.

"I get you're into her, and maybe she can bend you, but—"

"She's more than she looks," he said, then added, because he knew it would carry more weight with the werewolf, "or smells."

Malcolm shrugged. "It's your funeral. Come on then. We can change at my place. It's around the corner."

Malcolm lived in a deserted warehouse two blocks from the marina. From the outside, the place looked like it housed nothing but rats, spiders, and dust mites, but inside was a different story. TVs hung from the ceiling. Computers with flashing lights lined a wall. All the high-tech equipment made it look like a sound booth furnished with leather sofas and sleek chrome and glass tables. "I know what you're thinking...wondering really, but I have to tell you, money isn't an issue for me anymore."

"Why not?" Declan asked.

"Well, for one thing, I can't sleep, so I'm awake like all the time. I'm never tired. I can smell when someone's lying and when they're trying to hide something. So...you might laugh, but when anyone has stolen something, I take it back. They can't catch me." He pointed at Lizbet. "I know what you're thinking. You think I should return the stolen goods to the rightful owner. And that's what I do, if I can. But I also take a cut. A finder's fee, if you will–a small fraction for my trouble. And it is trouble. It's a risk. Plus, I'm constantly having to change my appearance. It's tiring."

"You're like Robin Hood," Lizbet said.

"Yeah, but I won't wear tights. Ever."

She smirked. "Right now, you're wearing a skirt."

He returned her smile. "But not for long. Excuse me and I'll get dressed."

Lizbet stepped closer to Declan as soon as Malcolm left the room. "Do you trust him?"

"Yeah, I do. Mostly because I don't think he trusts himself."

"Okay, then I guess I do too. It's interesting that even with all this easy money and the heightened senses and strength, he's not sure if this is what he wants."

"I think I'm starting to get it. It's like he didn't really earn it, like he was denied the fight. Does that make sense? He didn't really win, because there wasn't an even playing field. He got the trophy without having to play the game."

She followed his line of reasoning. "It's more like the rules of the game changed and he found he had been handed an advantage."

"Plus, it's a horrible thing to do to his parents," Declan said. "I wouldn't ever want to give up my family."

"But why do you have to?"

He shrugged. "From the way Malcom talks, the pack becomes your family."

Malcolm emerged from a back room wearing a pair of dark pants and a white shirt that offset his blue eyes. A shock of white hair replaced his long dark locks. "A wig," Malcolm told them. "I'm still hiding from the police, remember? But I'll be safe in the Wonderlust." He paused. "Well, as safe as I can be surrounded by wild dogs and bloodsuckers."

Chapter 9

Even with the new clothes, Lizbet felt underdressed because other than lip gloss and mascara, she wasn't wearing makeup. Declan assured her she looked beautiful.

"What is this place?" she asked as they walked to the door. Everyone was stunning, as if they'd leapt from the pages of a fashion magazine fully airbrushed. She tottered on her high heels and clung to Declan's arm. It struck her that he fit in perfectly, as did Malcolm. On the other hand, she did not. She was like homespun cotton surrounded by silk.

"You didn't tell her," Malcolm whispered.

Declan shook his head. "Not yet."

"Tell me what?"

"After we're inside," Declan said.

The doormen glared at them as they passed through the doors, but made no effort to stop them. Beside her, Declan gave a sigh of relief and his arm around her waist relaxed a fraction.

The club thrummed with heavy metal music. Couples moved in time on the dance floor. Crystal goblets and glass bottles in all shapes and sizes glistened on the shelves lining the walls. Declan led her to an empty table.

"Don't freak out," he whispered into her ear.

"You're saying that has pretty much guaranteed that I will," she said through clenched teeth. Her spine tingled with apprehension. There was something off about this place and these people. She couldn't put her finger on it, but if she had to guess she'd say they were too perfect, too beautiful, too...everything.

Declan held out a chair for her and she sank into it.

"There she is," Malcolm said, nodding at a stunning redhead dressed in cobalt blue on the other side of the club.

"Who's that?" Lizbet asked, not bothering to lower her voice since she doubted anyone could hear above the blasting music.

"Courtney Derringer," Declan told her.

A waitress glided up to them and without taking their orders placed goblets and a carafe of wine on the table. Lizbet thought about telling her they were underage, but bit her lip while Malcolm poured himself a glass.

"Missing Courtney? Why is she here when everyone is still looking for her?" Lizbet asked.

"She's a witch," Malcolm told her after sipping his drink.

"Well, yeah," Lizbet said. "This is a horrible thing to do to her parents, not to mention everyone else who cares about her."

"No, really, she's a witch," Malcolm said more slowly, as if she couldn't understand English and needed things spelled out more clearly.

"A witch. Like with a broomstick?"

"Why is that so hard to believe," Malcolm nodded at Declan, "when your boyfriend is a werewolf?"

Lizbet's world tilted. She had her own abilities, so why should she doubt others had gifts of their own? "Have you talked to her?"

"That's why we're here," Declan said. "Malcolm thinks she might be able to remove the curse."

"So being a wolf is a curse?" Lizbet asked.

"Hush!" Malcolm made a zipping motion across his lips. "Don't let anyone hear you say that," he hissed. "No one wants to believe they're a freak."

Lizbet bit her lip, because she understood him perfectly. Malcolm pushed away from the table, stood, and took another sip of wine before returning his goblet to the table. "I'm going to talk to her." He ran his hands over his hair, smoothing it down.

Lizbet leaned against Declan's shoulder. "Now are you going to tell me what's going on?"

Declan poured himself a drink.

Lizbet put her hand on his, stopping him. "Please don't. Somehow, I think we're both going to need to be thinking clearly tonight."

He nodded and set his goblet down. "You're right.

You wanted to know what this place is? It's a bar for paranormals."

"A what?"

He repeated himself.

"That's what I thought you said, it's just...that doesn't make sense. I don't think paranormals is even a word."

"The Wonderlust is a place where vampires, werewolves, witches, and sirens can meet and mingle."

"You're trying to make light of this, but I can tell you're only slightly less freaked out than me."

"I've had a little longer to process it."

Suddenly, a giant snarling tiger jumped onto the bar while a man transformed into a bat.

"Shape shifters," a gorgeous woman with silky blond hair at the next table sneered.

"And the vampire," her companion said. "I'm sure he's not blameless."

The doormen moved into the room, tossing over tables and chairs to reach the battling tiger and flying bat. A woman in a strapless black dress disappeared into a puff of smoke while her neighbor pointed at the bottles on the wall and sent them shattering into millions of shimmering shards. Lizbet felt her own composure cracking.

"Come on, let's get out of here." Declan reached for her hand.

Malcolm motioned to the back wall. Declan led her through the milling crowd to a side door. Outside, the

clean, cool air filled her lungs and she inhaled the scent of the nearby Sound.

"This place is crazy," Lizbet said. The hushed music still seeped through the walls, as did the noise of the battling paranormals.

"That? Oh, that's nothing," a female voice said. "I've seen it much, much worse."

Lizbet wheeled around, surprised. She hadn't seen Courtney and Malcolm in the shadowy alley. A lone lightbulb screwed into the far-end wall illuminated a row of nondescript doors.

Courtney elbowed Lizbet. "Malcolm explained the situation to me, and I'm happy to help."

"Do you think you can?" Declan asked.

"Well, I'm not sure it can hurt. Either it works or it doesn't. Of course, removing magic is much more difficult than inserting it, but I'm always eager to try something new." She sighed. "You'd be surprised how very few are willing to let me practice my magic on them. Everyone's so afraid of something going wrong. It's not as if spells can't be reversed."

"What about the dog-headed men?" Declan asked.

"Oh, those guys...they just suffer from indecision. They can't decide what they want, so they have to remain neither one until they reach a conclusion."

"Do you really think that's it?" Lizbet asked. "They have a choice?"

"Well, everyone has a choice, right?" Courtney said. She turned to Malcolm. "Are you sure about yours?"

Malcolm nodded. "I think so."

Frustration flashed across Courtney's face. "That's not a good enough answer! You have to know what you want for it to be manifested!"

"I want to be normal again," Malcolm muttered.

"Are you sure?" Courtney pressed.

Malcolm nodded.

"Okay, if you're really sure, I'll meet you at your place at midnight."

"Are you okay with my watching?" Declan asked.

"If you're considering it for yourself, I think it's a good idea," Courtney said.

Just then a cougar flew through the window, sending glass slivers spraying in all directions.

Courtney sighed and rolled her eyes. "Shape shifters!"

A somber mood filled the warehouse. The slap of water against pylons could be heard through the open window. Courtney lined up a variety of objects—a red candle on a brass stand, a tuft of fur, a knob of ginger—on the glass and chrome table.

"No skeptics." She pointed her finger at all of them as she gazed in each of their faces.

A flicker of dread crept through Lizbet. She didn't want to change Declan in any way. She loved him as he was. She tried telling herself that he had already changed, technically, and if he decided to go through with this, he would just be changing back to how he'd been before. She'd loved him then, too. But people were born to change. They went forward, not backward. As long as they remained healthy, they would evolve, not revert. Worry knotted in her belly, even though it was Malcolm asking to be reformed, not Declan. Still, it felt wrong to her.

"Everyone join hands and close your eyes," Courtney instructed.

Declan's grasp was strong and reassuring, while Courtney's hand felt cold and dry.

> *"Boundless courage, ceaseless strength, Goddess heed my name,*
> *Take him back to where he was before the curse upon him came."*

Claws scrambled on the hardwood floors and a dog yelped. Lizbet opened her eyes in time to watch a wolf dash through the window.

Declan chased after him, but he stopped at the sill. Lizbet peered over his shoulder at the dark water slapping the pylons. Any sign of Malcolm had completely disappeared.

Chapter 10

Declan beat Lizbet to the sidewalk. "I have to go after him," he told her.

She nodded. Her skin was raised with goose pimples and she shivered in front of him. He wanted to draw her into his arms and whisper in her ear that everything would be all right, but he also didn't want to lie.

"Where's Courtney?" Lizbet asked.

Declan gazed over the water where a silvery cloud moved faster than the gentle breeze. "I'm not sure," he said, his voice faltering. He ran his hands down Lizbet's trembling arms. "Listen, I think you should go."

She opened her mouth to protest, but he placed his finger on her lips.

"Please. I'll be faster without you."

"But I can help."

He glanced over his shoulder at the crowd gathered in front of the Wonderlust. Vampires, wolves, witches, sirens... Paranormals masquerading as beautiful but dangerous people.

"The animals—" Lizbet began.

He cut her off. "Do you see any around here?"

"No-oo," she said slowly.

"That's because they don't like werewolves, and because they're smart. They probably also have a healthy respect for and keep their distance from other...weirdos like me."

She opened her mouth to argue.

"I don't want to hear it," Declan said. "Please just go home. It's late. Make sure your mom sees you so you don't get in trouble."

"But what sort of trouble will you get in?"

Declan shrugged. "We'll have to see."

A blue light flickered through the living room windows, letting Lizbet know that her mom and maybe even her grandmother were awake and watching TV. John's car in the driveway told her that Declan's dad was also there.

Lizbet braced her shoulders and tried to smooth down her hair. She had a feeling that her expression would look as frazzled as her wild curls. It would be hard to look and act normal when life had taken such a sharp turn to the bizarre.

Monsters congregating in clubs. Vampires dueling with werewolves. Shape shifters. When had this become her world? She wanted nothing to do with these creatures, and yet, since Declan was one of them, she was guilty by association.

And who was to say she wasn't the strangest of them all? Until a few weeks ago, she had never heard of the Ollos Verdes, the green-eyed Native American tribe, and she was pretty sure the rest of the world was, for the most part, equally unaware.

Her feet dragged as she climbed the steps. The sound of canned laughter floated through the window, and she recognized the voices. They were watching Mr. Ed, a T.V. show about a talking horse. To them, and to most people, a talking horse was a preposterous idea. And yet, for Lizbet, she encountered talking horses, squirrels, birds, cats... everything every day.

She pushed open the door. Elizabeth sat in an easy chair with a quilt draped over her knees. She had her head tipped slightly back, her eyes closed, and her mouth open. Daugherty and John were curled together on the sofa. The laughter in their eyes dimmed as Lizbet walked in.

She waved, not wanting to interrupt their show.

"How was your night?" Daugherty asked.

"Good. We met up with some of Declan's friends in Seattle. Hung out." *Watched some dueling paranormals.*

Daugherty squinted at her. "Wow. Where'd you get the necklace?"

Lizbet's hand flew to the pendant on her chest. She'd changed out of her dress and put it in her backpack before getting on the motorbike, but had completely forgotten about the necklace. "Declan gave it to me."

Daugherty blinked. "It's stunning."

"I know, right?"

"Any special occasion?" her mom pressed.

"A graduation present."

"Huh. Did you give him one?" Daugherty asked.

"She doesn't need to give him anything," John spoke up. "That boy has everything he needs and more." He cleared his throat. "And where's my son now?"

Positive that John didn't want to hear about Declan chasing after a crazed young werewolf, she said, "I'm not really sure. He decided to stay with his friends. I have to work early tomorrow, so I came home."

John frowned at the TV screen. "What friends?"

"Malcolm and his girlfriend."

"Malcolm? The chess guy?" John scratched his head. "I didn't know he and Declan were friends."

"Isn't that the kid suspected of Jason Norbit's murder?" Daugherty sat up. "And the guard?"

An expression akin to terror crossed John's face.

"A different Malcolm," Lizbet said quickly, hating herself for lying so easily. "He's teaching Declan how to play chess." *And how to be a werewolf.*

Lizbet crossed the room and dropped a kiss on her

mom's cheek. "G'night." She thought about kissing Elizabeth, but decided not to wake her.

John and Daugherty echoed their goodnights.

Lizbet went to bed trying not to worry about Declan.

Declan stood beneath a glowing street light. A heavy mist hung in the air and fragmented the light into a shimmery haze. Lifting his nose to the air, he caught a whiff of wet dog tinged with the stink of fear.

A movement behind him made him glance over his shoulder. Courtney sat on the stone wall separating the sidewalk from the pier below. At first he thought she'd changed out of her blue dress, but then he realized she hadn't changed her clothes, but just the color of them. Her dress was now a blue-black—a color that blended seamlessly with the night sky. "Any luck?" she asked.

Declan shook his head.

She let out a shuddering sigh.

"How long have you been a witch?" Declan asked.

She lifted a shoulder. "I think I was born this way. It's been a..." She paused while she searched for the right words. "It's been hard on my parents," she finally said.

"How so?"

"They're devout Christians... They won't even read *Harry Potter*, because—according to them—all magic is the work of the devil."

"Wow. That's harsh."

"At first, we fought about it a lot." She rubbed her eyes. "I feel badly about the way I ended things. It was cruel—faking my kidnapping...but I was just so mad. And a part of me still thinks they deserve it."

Declan raised his eyebrows and waited for her to continue.

"They tried to brainwash the magic out of me. Sent me to a wilderness survival camp where we read from the Bible every day....that's the thing. They seem to have no problem with Moses parting the Red Sea, or Elijah riding into the sky in a chariot of flames, or a donkey talking to Balam, or...well, you get my point. I could go on and on."

"Do you see yourself ever reconciling with them?"

She lifted a shoulder. "I still have family. My grandmother is a witch. I learned everything I know from her."

"Did she teach you how to locate someone?"

A ghost of a smile crossed Courtney's lips as she shook her head. "You're the one with the nose." She looked around. "Do you think we should split up? It'll be faster."

Declan didn't answer her question because he had one of his own. "How did he change into a wolf?" He gazed up at the sliver of moon. This always reminded him of the grinning Cheshire Cat. "I mean, there's not a full moon."

Courtney cocked her head, staring at him. "You don't have to wait for a full moon. You can change any time you want."

Declan shivered. "Maybe Malcolm can, but I—"

"Have you ever tried it?"

"No..."

"You can control it, you know."

"I can?" His voice squeaked and he cleared his throat, hoping she hadn't noticed.

"Absolutely. You can control your body. It's as easy as flexing your fingers."

"How would you know?"

"I know a lot of wolves."

"And they can all change when and where they want?" She nodded.

He wanted to believe her, but he couldn't. He didn't have any say in the changes his body decided to make.

Courtney peeled herself off the wall and came to stand beside Declan. "Just close your eyes and imagine yourself as a wolf."

Declan shivered with repulsion. "I can't," he whispered.

Courtney took his hand. "You have to stop hating yourself."

"I don't..." His words trailed away, because he realized she was right. He didn't hate the person he knew as Declan, but he loathed and feared the wolf inside him.

"You have to make peace with this gift!" She shook his hand to emphasize her words.

"It's not a gift—it's a curse."

"Yeah. And it will be as long as you think it is. But if you can just wrap your mind around the amazing possibilities! Think of all the good you could do!"

"Good? Are you kidding me? For a while I thought I'd killed Jason. I even worried I had something to do with your disappearance."

"If you could learn to master your wolf, you'd find that you don't have any reason to be afraid of him."

A strange sense of ease flowed from Courtney's words. Declan shook himself and narrowed his eyes at her. "What are you doing?"

"What do you mean?"

The waves of peace and contentment washed over him. "You're doing something, aren't you? You're trying to put a spell on me."

She blinked. "No I'm not."

He pulled away from her reach. "Yes you are. Stop it." Feeling like he'd taken one too many Benadryls, he placed both hands on the sides of his head.

She laughed. "You're becoming more self-aware already." She elbowed him. "Come on, let's find Malcolm."

"Wait. If you really think I'm better off as a part-man part-wolf beast, why did you agree to change Malcolm?"

She smiled at him and comprehension dawned.

"What did you do?" he asked, his voice and thoughts thick with suspicion.

She batted her eyelashes. "Nothing."

"Yes you did. What was it?"

She sighed and stuck out her lower lip.

"Aren't you worried he'll do something…hurt someone?"

She laughed. "Malcolm? He can't hurt anyone."

"But as a wolf he might."

"No." She sounded so sure.

"How can you know that?"

"I know Malcolm. Violence isn't in his nature."

Declan felt a stirring of hope. "Do you think that's true of me as well?"

"That's completely up to you," she said.

"We should still go and look for him," Declan said.

Courtney raised her hand, palm up, and a small blue ball of light glowed.

Declan glanced around, worried what passersby might think, but they were alone on the sidewalk. He drew closer. Inside the ball, a miniature wolf loped through the woods.

"He's going home," Declan said.

"I have to stop him!"

"Wait. Why? Why is going home so bad?"

"It's not him I'm worried about. It's the police."

Of course. She was right.

"So, what are you going to do?"

"I want to take him to a colony in Alaska. There's a group of peace-loving paranormals there." She looked as if she wanted to say more, but waved her hands in the air and disappeared in a shimmery puff of silver.

Declan was alone.

When Declan crawled out of bed the next day, his whole body ached. The sun pouring through the window

told him he'd missed most of the morning. His dad's car in the driveway sent him a warning. He groaned. He was an adult. He could move out. Thanks to his inheritance from his grandfather, he was financially independent. He stayed for his mom. He loved his dad. And he knew that both of his parents loved him and that whatever they had to say to him would be said because they cared and were worried about him. But his body groaned from his night without sleep. Hunger tore at him. And guilt. He hated lying to his parents. But he didn't have a choice. The less they knew about the paranormal world, the safer and happier they'd be.

Before he headed downstairs to face the parental firing squad, he stepped into a pair of jeans and padded into the bathroom. He needed to shower, but he needed food more.

Although Gloria and John were somewhere in the kitchen using hushed voices, Declan could hear their every word while he ran the water to brush his teeth. Even though he didn't like or agree with the gist of their conversation, he had to admit that being a werewolf had its advantages. When his hunger could no longer be ignored, he made his way to the kitchen. His parents' conversation came to a stop when he entered the room.

"Declan, we need to talk," his dad said as he put down his coffee mug and pinned Declan with a steely glare.

"I know," Declan said as he pulled food from the fridge: a carton of eggs, a package of bacon, two red

peppers, a pound of cheddar cheese, a mozzarella ball, a bunch of spinach, an onion, some mushrooms, sausage, picante sauce, a pot of rice, a container of black beans. "You think I spend too much time with Lizbet."

His parents exchanged glances while he pulled out a frying pan, a cutting board, and a knife. He whacked his vegetables into small pieces.

"Lizbet told us you were with Malcolm—isn't he the kid who killed Jason and that deputy?" Gloria's voice squeaked with concern.

"A totally different Malcolm," Declan said. Sort of. He grabbed a bowl and began cracking eggs into it. "Either of you want an omelet?" He shot his parents a glance.

Gloria was frowning at him, while John stared at the mass of food on the counter.

"Good thing your dad left him all that money," John said to his ex-wife beneath his breath. "He's going to spend it all on food."

After pouring the vegetables onto the frying pan, he silently urged them to sauté faster. Keeping his eyes on the sizzling peppers, he went to the fridge to pour himself some orange juice. He tried not to choke on his impatience to be anywhere else.

"Hardly," Declan said. "Oh, I thought I'd try out for the UW basketball team. They have walk-on tryouts this morning." Knowing this would make them happy, he smiled at his parents' shocked faces.

"Huh, that's great, son." John cleared his throat. "I thought maybe you and I could go camping next weekend. Would you like that?"

Declan did some quick lunar counting, because the last thing he wanted was to spend a night in a tent with his dad as a werewolf. "Next weekend should be fine."

Gloria rubbed the back of her neck with her one operable hand. "You haven't been hanging around with Nicole, have you? Her parents are worried about her." There was a silent "also" at the end of that sentence, but Declan didn't comment on it.

"No, but it's understandable if she's acting differently," Declan said. "Her friend is missing, her boyfriend was murdered. Another kid—a good kid—that she knew from school killed a deputy. She has every right to be freaking out. It would be weird if she wasn't."

And because all those things could also be said of Declan, his parents fell silent as they waited for him to finish making omelets.

Declan's phone buzzed with a text and he pulled it out of his pocket.

COURTNEY: FOUND HIM
DECLAN: BE THERE AS SOON AS I CAN
COURTNEY: IT'S NOT SAFE. WAIT TIL DARK

Sacrifice your body. It had been a mantra Declan had grown up with. He couldn't remember a time when chasing balls or torturing them with sticks hadn't been a part of his daily routine. His dad, a football coach, had been an equal opportunity athlete. He hadn't pushed Declan into one sport, but had introduced him to most, if not all. Skiing in the winter, swimming in the summer, lacrosse, even polo and curling. In time, Declan had learned that most skills translated across the board. Speed, agility, coordination, teamwork...and the ability to sacrifice your body. Athletics, then—like any other pursuit—was a mind game first and a physical game second.

But on the University of Washington's basketball court where Declan was a walk-on, something strange was messing with his head. Voices. Where were they coming from and why did they ring in his ears?

To the left...

Under the basket...

Foul him...

Just like the morning when Declan had effortlessly flattened Baxter and winded McNally, he found it easy to outjump, out-rebound, and outrun the other players. Except for two: a tall dark man with arms like tree trunks and a feisty squat and square-shaped Asian. From outward appearances, nothing about them suggested an alliance, but they moved in sync as if their plays had been carefully choreographed beforehand.

It occurred to Declan that if he could hear their thoughts, they could possibly pick up on his as well. So he tried to keep his mind blank, which was surprisingly impossible to do.

An elbow in his gut. A shoulder bumping his arm. Flesh smacking flesh. The pound of feet. Palms slapping the ball. The stink of sweat and exertion tinged with desperation. The guy with tree-trunk arms passed Declan the ball. He caught it, dribbled down the court, blew past the other players, and sank a lay-up. It was a crap move. His dad would have told him that instead of showing off, he should have passed it off. Be a part of the team.

Only this was a team he didn't think he could play on. Not if there were pack members on it. He played halfheartedly, but finished out the scrimmage. It didn't surprise him when the Asian and the other guy cornered him in the locker room.

He smelled them before he saw them.

"Who are you?" The tall guy wore a friendly expression, but there was wariness behind his smile. He wore a towel around his neck and his skin glistened with sweat. He put one foot on the bench on one side of Declan while the Asian stood on the other. If the locker room hadn't been full of people, he would have felt intimidated, and it occurred to him that was exactly how they wanted him to feel.

Declan bared his own teeth, introduced himself, and followed it up with, "And you?"

"Gregson Nelson," the tall guy said.

"Lee Park," the Asian said.

The two exchanged glances. Declan tried to pick up on their thoughts, but drew a blank. Was it possible they could tune him out?

"We haven't seen you around," Lee said.

"Where'd you go to school?" Gregson asked.

"East End High. How about you?"

"Olympic Peninsula," Gregson answered for both of them.

"Things are wilder there," Lee said, lifting his chin.

"That's where all those girly Twilight books are set, right?" Declan tried to make it sound like a joke.

"Nothing girly about vampires," Gregson said.

"My mom and my sisters were so into that stuff," a guy next to them scoffed as he pulled on his jeans. "My mom dragged us all out to Forks when I was a kid. I can't believe you're actually from there." His gaze sized up Gregson and Lee before he tugged his T-shirt over his head.

"What is that supposed to mean?" Gregson asked in a dangerous tone.

"No offense...it's just not the most populated place."

Lee blinked. "We like it that way."

"Excuse me." Declan gathered up his backpack and headed out of the locker room.

"See you tomorrow?" Lee called after him. There was nothing menacing about the three words and yet they sounded like a threat.

Declan followed Courtney's directions to an abandoned warehouse in La Conner, a small out-of-the-way coastal town. The warehouse, a giant structure made up of corrugated tin, was held together by soaring wooden beams blackened with tar. Inside, away from the cool ocean breeze and weak moon, the air stank of kelp and brine.

Declan picked his way across the pocked cement floor. "Hello?" His voice echoed throughout the hollow space. A silvery bird darted in through a glassless window. For no good reason he could think of, he followed it to a dark corner where someone had parked a 1960s VW van.

The van's tires had long melted onto the floor. The side door gaped open, exposing a rusted metal floor. There was a driver's seat with curly springs poking through cracked vinyl behind the steering wheel and a lone bench in the back.

Malcolm and Courtney sat on the back bench. Malcolm had his hands between his knees while Courtney leaned away from him, her expression stony.

"I need you to convince him to go to Alaska," Courtney told Declan.

"I'm not running away," Malcolm said.

Courtney held up one finger. "One: the pack is hot to recruit you—and I don't have to tell you that they're not nice people...or creatures, or whatever they are." She lifted another finger. "Two: the police are after you—and they may or may not be nice people, but I'm pretty sure they won't be nice to you." She held up a third finger. "Three—"

Malcolm pushed her hand down. "I don't want to hear it, okay? I'm not ready to give up my life."

Courtney blew a loose strand of hair out of her face. "It's already gone. You're reduced to hiding in warehouses and gutted-out vans. What kind of life is this?"

"Where and how do you live?" Declan asked Courtney.

"I have everything I need—everything I could wish for... except for, you know, parental approval, a home, love..." Courtney said, her tone bitter.

"Thanks for proving my point." Malcom lifted his head and glared at her. "I've got to salvage my life somehow. I have to save it."

"I don't know what to do about the pack," Declan said, "but maybe if we could convince the police that you had nothing to do with Jason's death you could at least go home."

"It's too late for that," Courtney said.

"If I could just hide from the pack, I could at least hang around in Seattle...watch my family from afar."

"Would that be worth it?" Declan asked.

Malcolm nodded.

"Hiding from the pack is impossible!" Courtney said. "Hiding from humans is easy...transfiguration spells are a cinch...but hiding a smell from a werewolf is not going to happen."

Malcolm studied Declan. "I can't believe they haven't reached out to you."

Declan shrugged. "Should I feel excluded?"

"You're lucky!" Courtney said.

"You know what?" Malcolm said. "I don't need to hide from the pack—I need to get rid of them!"

"But how?"

"Wolfsbane!" Malcolm exclaimed.

"You're going to kill them? All of them?" Courtney asked.

"No...but I bet the threat of it could drive them away," Malcolm said.

Declan sat on the rusted floor. "Lizbet ordered some for the nursery."

"Yeah?" Courtney perked up.

"Mr. Neal wouldn't let her keep it. He said it was too toxic."

"So where is it now?" Malcolm asked.

Declan shrugged. "It's probably still there."

"You don't think he would have killed it?"

Declan shook his head. "Not a chance. Mr. Neal loves all his plants...even the deadly ones."

"Let's go and get it!" Courtney said.

"Huh...how are we going to do that?" Declan asked.

"Easy!" And with that, Courtney waved her hand and disappeared.

"Neat trick," Malcolm muttered. "So you're going to do it on your own?"

"No." Courtney's voice floated in the air. "I don't know my way around the nursery. Declan has to come with me."

"If you're taking him, you're taking me," Malcolm said.

"No need to get huffy," Courtney said seconds before Malcolm also disappeared.

Chapter 11

Declan, Courtney, and Malcolm stood inside Neal's Nursery parking lot waiting for Mr. Neal to leave.

Malcolm looked at his watch. "I keep forgetting I'm invisible," he said.

Declan looked at the sky, measuring the moon's distance to the horizon and trying to guess the hour.

"You wanted to be invisible," Courtney said. "I couldn't very well make your watch discernable...well, I could, but then you'd have a floating watch and that would be weird."

"He'll think it's weird if he hears us out here," Declan said under his breath.

"I think it's weird he hasn't left yet," Malcolm said. "He closed and locked the doors hours ago."

"Could he have gone out the back?" Courtney asked.

"Maybe..." Declan said.

"Let's just go in," Malcolm said. "He'll never notice us."

Declan showed them the back entrance. After typing in the code on the alarm, he pulled the gate open. It swung noiselessly on its hinge. But another noise came from inside the office. Strains of *Mozart's Requiem in D Minor* floated through the air like the soundtrack of a horror movie.

Declan bumped into Malcolm.

"Watch it!" Malcolm hissed.

"How can I watch you?" Declan whispered. "You're invisible. Why'd you stop?"

"Mozart died listening to this," Malcolm said.

"How is that even possible?" Courtney whispered. "Did he have an orchestra and a choir at his deathbed?"

"Probably not, but it's still creepy," Malcolm said. "They also claim that Mozart received the commission from a mysterious messenger who wouldn't reveal the commissioner's identity. Mozart believed he was writing the requiem for his own funeral."

Courtney sighed. "Are you trying to spook us?"

Declan pulled his phone from his pocket and used his flashlight function. "Guys, this way." He led them to the corner farthest from the office. Ducking behind the shelter of potted fruit trees, Declan searched for images of wolfsbane on his phone. "This is what we're looking for." His phone looked as if it floated midair.

"Oh, it's pretty," Courtney said.

"Doesn't look so deadly," Malcolm said.

"That's part of its power," Courtney told him.

"Let's split up," Malcolm said.

"It's not out here," Declan said. "Mr. Neal told Lizbet they couldn't sell it."

"So—where is it?" Malcolm asked.

"Probably in the office." Declan turned off his phone and slipped it back into his pocket.

"But that's where Neal is!" Malcolm said.

"We can wait for him to leave," Courtney said.

"Smart...but boring," Malcolm said.

"Do you have a better idea?" Courtney asked.

When no one said anything, Declan touched their arms so they'd follow him. They crept down the sawdust-strewn path between the ferns and hydrangea. When they got to the office, they peeked in the window. Mr. Neal sat slumped in his chair, his head back, and his mouth and eyes open.

"Oh no, Mr. Neal!" Declan cried.

"Is he dead?" Courtney asked.

"I would say so," Malcolm said.

Declan blinked back tears. He'd always liked his former boss. Pushing past his friends, he entered the office and stood in the center of the room. If this was soon to be a murder scene, he didn't want to leave his fingerprints on anything. But what if Mr. Neal wasn't dead? Although, he certainly looked it...

"Do you think it was suicide?" Courtney asked.

"No." Declan shook his head. "Absolutely not." He

stiffened his spine and knelt beside Mr. Neal and reached for his wrist. He was already cold. When Declan didn't feel a pulse, he placed his two fingers on Mr. Neal's throat. Definitely no pulse.

"Maybe a heart attack," Malcolm suggested.

"Okay, guys, this is terrible—but here's a thought," Courtney began. "What if we write a suicide note claiming that—"

"No!" Declan stood, unable to take his gaze off Mr. Neal.

"Why not? It will get Malcolm off the hook!" Courtney said.

"But his family, they deserve to know the truth," Malcolm said.

"Mr. Neal didn't have any family." Declan sucked in a deep breath. "But he was a great guy. Everyone loved him."

Malcolm looked at the ceiling. "As much as I would love to go home to my family, I can't... I won't shift the blame to an innocent man. Even if he's dead."

Courtney's shoulders sagged. "You're right. What we need to do is make the real murderers pay."

"There's no way for that to happen," Malcolm said.

Declan eyed a flat of ragweed. "Maybe we can't pin Jason's murder on the pack, but we can make at least a few of them miserable."

"How exactly does this work?" Lizbet asked Courtney the next day as they stood in the deserted UW quad outside

the locker room. The first day of fall semester was only a few weeks away and since the summer term had ended, the campus held an eerie stillness. The sound of thumping basketballs came from the nearby gym's open windows.

Courtney flushed. "I can't tell you how it works, I can only promise you that it does."

"But the plants?"

"Yes, they'll look like they're floating through the air, unless we can tuck them under our shirts or something."

Lizbet shook her head. "That's a really, really bad idea."

Courtney looked out over the quad. Other than a lone girl sitting on a stone bench, hunched over her phone, and a gardener raking the leaves from a flowerbed, they were alone. "Well, I'm not too sure about this plan, either." She turned her frown on Malcolm. "Why did we think this was a good idea?"

"It's payback," Malcolm muttered.

"But we don't even know if these wolves on the basketball team had anything to do with Jason's death," Courtney said.

"Just the fact that they're still in school says a lot about them," Lizbet said.

"You're right," Malcolm said. "Most of the wolves drop out. But still...the wolves operate as a pack. They're incredibly symbiotic."

"But we're not punishing the pack," Lizbet pointed out. "We're singling out only a couple of them."

Malcolm pointed a finger at Lizbet's chest. "If you

had any idea how miserable they have made my life, we wouldn't be having this conversation. But I totally get it if you don't want to be involved."

Lizbet bit her fingernail. She wanted to help them because they were friends of Declan's, but she disagreed with their tactics—even though Declan had insisted the plan had been his. She handed the carton holding the ragweed to Malcolm before stripping off her leather gloves.

"I'll wait out here and keep watch," Lizbet said. "Don't even think about handling the plants without using the gloves," she told Courtney. Turning to Malcolm, she added, "And that means you can do nothing but carry the box."

"We need some sort of signal if someone comes in," Malcolm said.

Lizbet took note of the nearby animals. A robin sat in a birch tree. A wren worked on his nest in the gym's eaves. A squirrel scurried through a flowerbed. "If a bird or an animal comes in, that means someone is coming."

Courtney narrowed her eyes at Lizbet. "How are you going to get an animal to go in the locker room?"

"You have your tricks, and I have mine," Lizbet said.

She followed them to the locker room door, pulled it open, and stuck her head inside. It reeked, but was empty.

Courtney nodded at Malcolm. Moments later they disappeared and the carton of ragweed floated midair.

"Good luck," Lizbet whispered before closing the door on them.

Wandering back outside, she pulled a piece of bread out of her pocket and went to make friends with the robin—just in case she needed back-up.

"I really want to stay and watch," Declan said after he emerged from the locker room.

Lizbet shook her head. "It's not safe. Do you think they were successful?"

"I have no idea," Declan told her. He ran his fingers through his wet hair. His shirt clung to his still-damp skin, and he smelled of soap and shampoo. He slung his gym bag over his shoulder. "Have you seen them?"

"No, but they *are* invisible."

His lips quirked in a smile. "It's pretty cool being friends with a witch."

"And I bet you're a star on the basketball court."

"Don't forget there's a couple of other creatures there, too." His grin widened. "But, yeah, I'll make the team." His smile faded slightly. "That wouldn't have been a guarantee a few weeks ago." He paused. "It seems like cheating now. Besides, I'm not so sure I even want to be on it anymore."

"Don't forget there's a downside as well as the upside. I mean it's not as if you made the choice."

Declan pressed his lips together. "I would still go back

if I could... Being a monster, it's not something I would wish on anyone."

"But since going back isn't a choice, doesn't it make sense to make the best of it?" Lizbet asked.

He slung his arm over her shoulder and kissed her temple. "Absolutely." His back pocket buzzed with an incoming text. He pulled out his phone. "It's Courtney. She wants us to meet them at the Wonderlust at eight."

Lizbet flinched beneath Courtney's frown. "That's the same dress you wore the last time," Courtney said, raising her voice to be heard over the steady beat of the classic rock blaring from the speakers suspended from the ceiling of the Wonderlust club.

Lizbet glanced around at the crowd. Like Courtney, everyone in the bar wore a supernatural beauty. Lizbet doubted that anyone would even give her a second glance. "I don't think anyone will notice."

Courtney rolled her eyes and lifted her hand. "Do you mind?" she asked.

"Huh, no?" Lizbet wasn't sure what she was agreeing to, but in a flash, her blue dress was transformed into a silver sequin-studded sheath.

"Wow," Malcolm breathed.

The look in Declan's eyes told Lizbet he agreed.

Malcolm motioned for them to sit at a corner table. Lizbet weaved through the crowd following the others, feeling increasingly out of place. Glancing around, she wondered if she were the only human in the room and if her ordinariness was as obvious to others as it was to her. She felt as if she wore a neon sign declaring her a human.

"Where did you guys go this afternoon?" Declan asked as they settled into a red, crushed velvet booth.

Courtney's eyes sparkled and she folded her arms and leaned across the table. "We had to watch the itch fest," she said in a barely audible voice.

"You should have seen it," Malcolm said. "It was hilarious."

Courtney elbowed him. "Hush. We can't let anyone know it was us."

"We rubbed the plants into their underwear," Malcolm said.

"Which was more than a little gross," Courtney said.

"We were wearing gloves," Malcolm told her.

"But still..." She shuddered.

"Just their underwear?" Lizbet asked.

"I wanted to do all of their clothes, but we ran out of time," Malcolm told her.

"We were interrupted by a janitor," Courtney said.

"Did he see you?" Lizbet asked.

Both Courtney and Malcolm shook their heads. "At least we don't think so," Courtney added.

"We got the most important parts," Malcolm said with a smirk. "You have never seen so much contorting."

"Or heard so much howling," Courtney added. Her smile faded. "What's happening with Mr. Neal?"

Declan shrugged. "I hated to just leave him there, but I'm sure someone must have found him by now."

"What are you talking about?" Lizbet asked, her gaze flashing from Courtney to Declan. "What do you mean, someone would find Mr. Neal?"

Declan paled. "Geesh, I'm sorry, Lizbet. I should have told you. Mr. Neal is dead."

"What?"

Declan put his hand on hers, trying to steady her. "We found him at the nursery. He probably had a heart attack."

"And you're just telling me now?"

Declan squeezed her hand. "I'm sorry. I know you liked him."

"Of course I liked him! I thought you did, too."

"I do! I mean I did."

"But you just left him there without getting any help?"

"What were we supposed to do?" Malcolm asked. "We weren't supposed to be there. We were invisible."

"What if he wasn't dead? What if it had been just a stroke or something?"

"He was cold... He didn't have a pulse."

"But still! Mr. Neal!" Lizbet pulled her hand out of Declan's grasp. "I can't... I can't be here right now."

Standing, she tried to stalk away, but could only totter on her shimmery high heels.

Declan moved to follow her.

She stopped him. "Just give me a moment."

It took her a long time to move through the crowd. Someone grabbed her bottom, a pale woman with long silver hair jostled her, a man with crimson lips and amber eyes leered at her. Was this where Declan now belonged? The thought made her breath catch.

Outside, the cool, damp air filled her lungs. Leaning against the building, she pulled off one shoe and then the other. With her feet firmly on the ground, she felt more like herself. She cast a glance over her shoulder, worried that Declan would follow. She couldn't talk to him right now.

How could he be so heartless about Mr. Neal? She followed the sidewalk into a shadowy alley and took a seat at a step leading to a cigar shop's back door. The smell of tobacco filled her head while tears gathered in her eyes.

Mr. Neal had given her a job when no one else would because she didn't have a social security number. He'd taught her to love Mozart, Beethoven, and Bach and helped her realize that the plants had feelings, too.

And right now, she wondered if Declan had any feelings at all.

"Hey, pretty, why so sad?" a voice asked in the dark.

Lizbet glanced around, but she couldn't see anyone. Who had followed her and why? She stood, looked right and left. Something fluttered above her head, ruffling

her hair. Glancing up, she caught sight of black wings. Something tapped her on the shoulder. Whirling, Lizbet stumbled back just as a fist slammed into her face.

Pain exploded in her jaw and her vision blurred. She landed hard on her butt. Her head banged against the cigar shop's door.

"Wait. Are you sure she was with them?"

She looked up, trying to focus despite the confusion and pain engulfing her. A tall lanky man hovered over her. She wondered if he had been one of the basketball players Declan had talked about.

"Why would those wolves hang with an ordinary thing like her?" the same voice asked.

The lanky man swung his foot and kicked Lizbet in the chest. She rolled away and curled into a tight ball as agony rippled through her.

Someone grabbed a handful of her hair. Lizbet mustered her remaining strength and screamed.

Footsteps pounded down the alley. The hand entangled in her hair released her.

A voice chuckled. "Now we got ourselves a real dog fight!"

The sickening sound of flesh hitting flesh filled Lizbet's head. She uncurled, and tried to lift her head, but pain kept her down.

The sounds changed. Snarling replaced words. When Lizbet managed to raise herself to her elbows, she saw four wolves embroiled in a fight filled with fur, blood, and saliva.

Every part of Lizbet ached. She cracked open an eye and was surprised to find herself in her bed. Her closet doors gaped open and the silvery dress hung on the rod. The only telltale sign of the previous night's trouble was that one of the silver shoes had lost its heel. The shoe lay on its side on the closet floor like a toppled tree.

Pain screamed through her when she tried to move, making her wonder if her rib was broken.

"*What happened to you?*" Tennyson asked.

"Dogs," Lizbet said through dry and cracked lips, knowing that because of the cat's absolute hatred of the species, he would need no further explanation. She crawled from her bed and stood on wobbly legs. After tottering to the mirror hanging above her dresser, she gaped at her reflection. She had expected to find her face looking as bruised and battered as she felt, but her skin was as flawless as always. She ran her fingertips over her lips. In the mirror they appeared perfect... This, she decided, had to be Courtney's work. A witch was much more skilled than a plastic surgeon.

As if thinking of her could conjure her, Courtney appeared in the center of the room amid a haze of silvery light.

Tennyson sprang to his paws with a hiss.

"It's okay," Lizbet whispered, climbing back onto her bed and gathering her cat into her arms. She wanted to

sound reassuring, but she heard the fear in her own voice. She stroked the cat.

"Sorry for barging in on you like this," Courtney said as soon as she fully materialized.

Tennyson jumped from Lizbet's arms and bolted out the open window.

"Chicken," Lizbet murmured, even though she pretty much wanted to do the same thing.

"Declan is frantic about you." Courtney strode across the room, picked up Lizbet's phone from the bedside table and pressed buttons. "You need to keep this charged." She waved the phone at Lizbet before settling down on the bed beside her and studying her. "How are you?"

Lizbet shrugged and tried to look brave.

"Pretty freaked out?" Courtney pressed.

Lizbet stared at her feet. "I don't know if I can do this," she whispered. "I love Declan, but I don't want to be a part of this world."

Courtney bumped Lizbet's shoulder with her own. "Remember, being a werewolf wasn't something Declan signed up for, either."

"I know, but..."

"Besides, paranormals are a part of this world no matter what. You can ignore us and pretend we're not here...but the truth is, we *are* here. We always have been. And we're not going away."

Lizbet swallowed. "I liked things better when I didn't..."

"Feel threatened?"

Lizbet nodded. "I want to hate the werewolves, but the truth is, I don't totally blame them. After all, we did—"

Courtney stood. "No. They absolutely deserved what they got and worse. They killed Jason Norbit! And framed Malcolm. They've ruined his life. Not to mention Declan's! And they killed his grandfather and the nurse." She clenched her fists. "We're not the only ones who hate the werewolves. They're considered the scrubs of the paranormal world. But I have an idea. Declan and Malcolm are already on board with it. I think we need to enlist the help of the other paranormals."

Lizbet wanted to do nothing more than put a pillow over her head and ignore the rest of the world, but since Courtney looked so determined, she tried to look mildly interested.

"And we're in luck! There's a circle meeting tonight."

Lizbet did not see how luck factored into anything. "A circle?"

"Of witches."

"Like a coven?"

Courtney sighed. "There's a lot of debate on that. Technically, a coven can only have nine or thirteen members and those members tend to adhere to the same practice of magic."

"There are different ways to practice magic?"

"Of course."

"But I'm not a witch. Are you sure they'll want to include me in their circle?"

"Frankly, I think there are a good many wannabes in the circle—although no one would ever call them that. This circle is pretty open. Witches tend to be free spirits and—as a rule—they shun hierarchy or pride of any kind. They'll be very welcoming, not because of who you are, but more because any sort of exclusivity or elitism violates their values."

"What...how...why?"

"Don't you see? We'll ask the witches to help us drive the werewolves from the area!"

Lizbet tucked her arm around her bent knees. "How are they going to do that?"

"They're witches! I'm sure they'll have some ideas."

"How long have you been a witch?"

"I've always been a witch. I was born a witch...as all witches are. We can't be turned like vampires or werewolves."

Lizbet thought Courtney sounded on the verge of boasting. "Yes, but how did you become a witch? Is it something you can work towards?"

"No. Don't be silly. No one gets to choose their lineage."

"So, it's as if a witch-born has scored a goal in a match that mere mortals aren't allowed to play in?"

Courtney blinked. "I've never thought of it like that. But you're right. When it comes to becoming a witch, no one climbs a ladder, checks off tasks on a to-do list, or fulfills a list of requirements. Becoming a full-fledged

coven member is dependent on one thing only—your blood. It's either in you, or it isn't."

"So, how do they know if you have the right blood or not? I bet some people think they're witches—or want to be witches—and they're just not."

"I don't know everything." Courtney nodded. "I'm new."

"But I thought you said you were born a witch?"

"I was—eighteen years ago. And I've only been practicing for a few months. That makes me young—like infantile young. A lot of the sisters—that's what we call each other—in the coven have been practicing for centuries. That's why asking the coven for a favor scares me." She braced her shoulders. "But I'm not just asking for myself. Besides, I can't think of any other creature that doesn't hate the wolves as much as witches."

"That's gotta be rough on the wolves," Lizbet said.

"We can't feel sorry for them!" Courtney said. "We have to get rid of them!" She paused and looked at Lizbet. "Are you in?"

"Of course, but—"

"No buts! I'll pick you up at a quarter to midnight."

Lizbet nearly stumbled over her grandmother sitting at the kitchen table in the dark. Elizabeth had her head buried in her arms and Lizbet couldn't tell if she was

asleep, awake, or... "What's the matter, Grandma?" Lizbet asked.

When Elizabeth slowly raised her head, a whoosh of relief washed over Lizbet.

"I just don't know what's going to happen, child," Elizabeth said.

Lizbet put her hand on her grandmother's shoulder and glanced at the clock. She had about ten minutes before Courtney would pick her up. She desperately wanted Elizabeth safely tucked in bed by then. She didn't have time for a heart to heart, and that made her feel guilty. Her grandmother had given her so much—shelter, both physical and emotional, food, guidance. After a quick glance out the window at the rising moon, Lizbet asked, "What do you mean?"

"Your aunt thinks I'm too old to be living here on my own...and sometimes I think she's right."

Lizbet dropped into a chair beside her grandmother and clasped Elizabeth's hand in hers. "But you're not on your own. I'm here. My mom's here. We're not going to leave you or the ranch."

Elizabeth raised her red-rimmed eyes to meet Lizbet's gaze. "But you should! You should go to school. Daugherty should marry John!"

Lizbet laughed. "I think that's up to my mom and John."

"And you should go away to college! Have adventures!"

"I'd rather stay here."

"You don't mean that."

Lizbet squeezed her grandmother's hand. "But I do." An idea clicked. "And I can prove it to you!"

"Now, how—"

Lizbet jumped to her feet. "Wait right here. I'll show you." She ran to her room and returned moments later with a bottle of blackberry wine.

"What's this?" Elizabeth asked.

"This is magic, pure and simple," Lizbet said, and she pulled a glass out of the cupboard. "Although it doesn't always work. I hope tonight it will, for your sake." She set the glass and bottle in front of her grandmother. "This is Matias and Maria's mawmaw's wine. But don't worry. It's not really alcoholic. I don't know why they call it that." She filled the glass. "But it is...amazing. Although not always."

"What does it do?" Elizabeth picked up the glass with a shaky hand.

"Sometimes...it will show you glimpses of the future."

"I'm not sure I want to see my future. I don't have much of one left and I'm terrified Josie is going to stick me away in a home."

"I think if you just take a swallow of this, you'll see how much my mom and I love living here with you."

"Are you sure?" Elizabeth asked.

"Absolutely," Lizbet said. "We're not going anywhere." She kissed her grandmother's cheek and prayed for Mawmaw's magic to happen before Courtney arrived.

Elizabeth raised her eyebrows and tilted the glass to her lips while Lizbet waited.

After a long moment, Lizbet asked, "So, what did you see?"

"It was a memory." Elizabeth gave her a dreamy smile. "I saw your grandpa. He looked so handsome...so young. He was holding out his hand to me and there was music playing."

"Were you young, too?"

"I was." She looked into the now-empty glass as if she expected it to tell her something. "You know, I don't feel old on the inside. In my head, I'm still that young girl your grandpa fell in love with. It's only when I try to get up on a horse, or plant the tomatoes, or a million and one other things that make my body creak that I'm reminded that I can no longer do the bunny-hop without getting wheezy."

Lizbet squeezed her grandmother's hand. "Well, I love you, no matter how wheezy you get."

A dense, cottony fog hung in the trees. A few owls called out to Lizbet as she followed Courtney into the state park. "Don't witches get cold?" Lizbet asked.

"Are you cold?" Courtney threw a glance over her shoulder.

Lizbet huddled into her jacket and tried to forget about the warm bed she'd left behind. The path weaved in front of them, twisting through trees and tangled bushes full of thorns and stickers. Her body ached from her beating. Even though the physical wounds weren't obvious, the emotional trauma ran deep. She twitched at every snapping twig. Her skin prickled with apprehension and goosebumps pimpled her arms and legs. If she were an insect, her antennas would be waving in the air, searching for danger.

A lone figure sat on a fallen log, her face shadowed by the hood of her dark cape. As they approached, she uncurled from her perch.

"You're late," she said without a greeting.

Courtney stiffened. "I didn't know I was expected."

The woman chuckled. "You thought you could take us by surprise?"

"No..." Courtney's voice faltered. "But I had hoped... Do you know why I've come?"

The woman, draped in black, was neither beautiful nor ugly. Her face had an ageless appearance, and her cloak covered her head to toe, but she carried herself as if she were royalty. The only remarkable thing about her was the staff she carried. It was blacker than the night sky and shaped like a snake. The handle was carved like a head and two glowing rubies formed the eyes. Lizbet couldn't help staring at it.

The woman inclined her head. "It's not an unreasonable request. There have been many in the past who have asked the same."

A rustling behind her drew Lizbet's attention to the largest black cat she'd ever seen trailing behind them.

"The circle will listen to your request, mostly out of respect for your grandmothers," the woman said. "I would fain be friends with you, for their sake."

"You knew my grandmothers?"

The woman nodded again. "Back in Salem."

"My grandmothers didn't live in Salem. One lived in Portland and the other in Everett. Grandma Littleton wasn't a witch. She was the president of her church council and taught kindergarten for nearly fifty years."

The woman chuckled. "You don't think a church council president and a kindergarten teacher can be a witch? Reconsider."

Moon glow filled the small clearing where the witches gathered. Some were Hollywood beautiful, but most wore the same nondescript face as the woman who had earlier joined them. Many hovered a few inches off the ground and floated more than stood. As if on cue, although Lizbet hadn't noticed one, the witches formed a circle. One voice started singing, but soon everyone but Lizbet had joined the chorus. The wind howled in tune, and the trees swayed in time. Somewhere close, a river rushed. Beasts howled, chattered, and clicked. It seemed as if all of nature sang along in praise of the earth, the moon, and the magic.

Chapter 12

When the singing ended, silence filled the valley as the witches bowed their heads. Even the noises from the wind, animals, and nearby stream fell still.

"What's happening now?" Lizbet whispered to Courtney.

Courtney responded by pressing a finger to her lips and lowering her head. "Pray." She mouthed the word.

Lizbet bowed her head and scrambled to string coherent thoughts together. *Please help us to get home safely when this is over. Please bless the witches to help us.*

"Sister Price will now read our notes from our last meeting," a woman said, breaking the silence.

Lizbet raised her eyebrows in question, but Courtney didn't seem to find this at all surprising.

Sister Price, a small, round woman—who, aside from her black cape, looked like she'd be more at home behind the library circulation desk than in a witches' meeting in a midnight forest—stepped into the center of the circle and cleared her throat.

"Notes from the meeting held on August first," she began, holding a small notepad in front of her. "Sister Pickering suggested we hold this year's celebration of All Hallows' Eve in the town cemetery as opposed to the St. John's cemetery." She read without raising her eyes to the witches floating around her.

A discontented murmur stirred through the crowd.

"But we've always held our celebration at the St. John's cemetery!" a witch spoke up.

"This is exactly why Sister Pickering thought a move would be a good idea," Sister Price said. "Isn't that right, Matilda? We want things to be fair."

Matilda Pickering stepped forward. With the cloak around her shoulders, she looked almost as wide as she was tall. "There's more to it than that," she said. "There's also the convenience factor. As you know, the St. John's cemetery has fallen into disrepair—"

"Which only adds to its appeal!" a witch from the crowd chimed in.

"Yes, it's wonderfully isolated," another witch chimed in.

"But it's hard to find. I get lost every year," one of the few witches standing on the ground complained.

"Get a GPS," a witch in the back said with a growl.

Lizbet glanced at the moon. It smiled down on her like the Cheshire Cat. She swayed on her feet with fatigue and

her thoughts strayed to Declan. He would be safe for a few more weeks. But after that? What about when school started? She tried to imagine him sitting through pre-med courses after a night of roaming the woods. What would it be like to take classes prepping him to save lives when he feared he'd been responsible for taking them? Her eyes flew open when Courtney began to speak.

"As I'm sure you're all aware, the werewolf problem has gotten out of hand," Courtney said.

A murmur of discontent ran through the crowd.

"She's right! We shouldn't have to put up with the fur balls and their shenanigans!" one witch said.

"But they have as much right as any to be here," another said.

"They're endangering all paranormals!"

"They'll expose us for sure!"

Sister Price pounded her staff on the ground for attention. "Sisters!"

"I have an idea." Sister Pickering stepped forward again.

Sister Price scowled at her. "Well, let's hear it then."

"We'll help only if we can get the vampires on board," Sister Pickering suggested.

"The vampires?" a witch squeaked.

"Ha! That will never happen!" another said.

"Well, it couldn't hurt to ask," someone said.

"Yes it could," another answered. "It could hurt a great deal!"

Sister Price held up her hands, asking for silence. A hush fell. "Are you willing to try to recruit the vampires to your cause?" she asked Courtney.

Courtney nodded. "We're in luck! The vampires hold their annual festival in North Corner."

"It's your funeral," a witch said.

"How will we find the vampires?" Lizbet whispered.

"Easy, we wait for lightning," Courtney whispered back. "Come on, let's go and tell the boys our plan."

Chapter 13

This isn't a plan," Malcolm said. "This is suicide."

Declan and Lizbet sat side by side on a sofa in Malcolm's warehouse. Declan kept his fingers wound through Lizbet's as he watched Malcolm and Courtney argue.

"Didn't it occur to you that if you asked the vampires and witches to drive out the werewolves, we—" he waved his finger between himself and Declan "—would also have to leave."

Lizbet could see from the look on Courtney's face that she hadn't thought of this.

Lizbet wanted to hit herself on the forehead, because she should have realized this as well. "It's just so hard to think of you as werewolves," she said in a hushed tone.

"Well, we are," Malcolm said.

Declan slid a quick glance at Lizbet and cleared his throat. "What does lightning have to do with vampires?"

Courtney waved her hand in the air. "Oh nothing, it's just..."

Malcolm stood and began to pace. "The vampires gather during thunderstorms. And, as you know, thunderstorms are common at the end of the summer on the eastern side of the Cascades."

Courtney nodded. "That's where we could find the vampires."

"If we wanted to find the vampires," Malcolm added.

"I still don't understand," Lizbet said.

"According to Slavic mythology, there's an ongoing battle between Perun, god of thunder and lightning, and Veles, the horned black god of the underworld." Malcolm sat on the edge of the sofa and silently tapped his foot.

"He's the leader of the vampires," Courtney said.

"When Perun gets fed up with Veles and his vampires, he starts throwing lightning bolts. Veles and his minions taunt Perun by transforming themselves into various animals and hiding behind trees, houses, even people," Malcolm said. "Ultimately, Perun hopes to defeat Veles and the vampires and return them to the realm of the dead."

Courtney added, "We think of summer storms as signs of the changing of the seasons, but actually they're just supernatural battles."

"The storms can sometimes get really out of control," Malcolm said.

Courtney nodded. "Like the storm of 1903."

"What happened?" Lizbet asked.

"It was in a small farming town called Mapleton in northeastern Washington," Malcom began. "People went to church, ate dinner, and relaxed with family and friends. But late that afternoon, what everyone thought was a

violent thunderstorm hit the town with heavy rain and hail, soaking the mountains and bare hills bordering the town.

"The thunder and pounding hail masked the sound of something they likely could not have imagined: a roaring two-story wall of water raging toward town. Within an hour, one of every five people in the town of thirteen hundred would lose their lives as the flood pulled apart and carried away nearly everything in its path. The center of town was devastated. Enormous drifts of debris, tangled around bodies, snaked down the valley."

"If the vampires are busy battling Perun, chances are they're not going to have time to listen to us," Declan said.

"It's a bad plan, anyway," Malcolm said. "Like I said, even if we could get the vampires to drive out the wolves—they'd want to send us, too."

"I've been thinking," Declan said slowly. "Maybe leaving is the best idea."

"Declan, no!" Lizbet tightened her grip on his hand.

"Look, we want the wolves to leave," Declan said, "because we think everyone will be safer without them. Well, that includes me—" he paused and looked at Malcolm "—and you."

"You're right." Malcolm pushed to his feet. "It's a decision I've been fighting for weeks. I think I'm ready to go."

"If you're going, I'm going," Courtney said.

Declan looked at Lizbet. She gave a small shake of her head. "I can't," she said, her voice faltering as she

remembered her promise to Elizabeth. She had said she wouldn't leave. How could she go with Declan when Elizabeth needed her help on the ranch? Biting her lower lip, she sent a prayer to heaven that somehow, someway, she'd be able to keep her promise to Elizabeth and not be separated from Declan.

Declan took Courtney and Malcolm to the train station first thing in the morning. "I still don't get why you need a train," Declan said.

"What do you mean?" Courtney asked as they stood in the ticket line.

"Why not just teleport?" Declan asked.

A business man carrying a briefcase flashed Declan a startled look.

"I'm joking, of course," Declan told the man. "And you shouldn't listen to other people's conversations."

The man grunted before he turned his attention to the lady on the other side of the counter.

"I can do short distances pretty easily," Courtney told him. "But things can get sketchy if I try to push myself. Besides, using my magic always drains me. I'm afraid if I tried to teleport myself to Alaska, I could end up in Zimbabwe and so weak I wouldn't be able to correct the situation for weeks. And who knows where Malcom could end up."

The business man stared at Courtney.

"Sir," the woman behind the counter addressed him, "your tickets."

The man shook himself, grabbed the tickets, turned on his heel, and hurried away.

"I hope we don't sit by him on the train," Malcom said.

"He won't recognize us even if we do," Courtney said before turning to the woman behind the counter. "Two tickets for Blaine."

As previously arranged, they'd take the train to Blaine, and from there sneak across the border into Canada and then carry on to the colony of peaceful paranormals living in Alaska who would provide them a safe harbor.

Today, Malcolm was back in his feminine Goth clothes while Courtney wore a trench coat and fedora and carried a leather satchel. She'd need a coat where they were headed. Malcolm not so much. They stood beneath a ticking clock, their faces resolute and yet scared.

His heart ached for both of them. They hadn't asked for this. They were both good kids, A students, they'd done everything right. Taken the AP classes. Played in the band and orchestra. Provided the community service. And yet, here they were, about to get on a train that would lead them to a life they hadn't prepared for and couldn't have ever imagined.

Declan hugged them both goodbye. As he watched them board the train, he couldn't help wondering if he would soon follow.

"You don't have to come with me," Declan said, sounding miserable.

"I've always wanted to see the northern lights." Lizbet bumped her shoulder against his, trying not to think of her promise to Elizabeth.

"The light here is pretty cool..."

They sat side by side on a blanket overlooking Elinor Bay. The sun, a smudge of light peeking through low clouds, hung on the horizon.

"But what will you do?" Declan cleared his throat. "What will I do?"

"I don't think we need to do anything drastic...after all, Godwin was able to live a fairly normal life as part man, part wolf."

"Godwin is not my role model."

"I get that, but I just think that if he can do it—you can, too."

"But he has a pack... Like Nicole said, no one likes a lone wolf."

Lizbet shifted and looked over her shoulder as if she expected to see Nicole. Instead, she saw an elderly man walking a greyhound, a young couple pushing a double stroller, and a man on a nearby bench listening to something on his phone...normal people leading normal lives. Or so she thought. But what did she really know? For all she knew, every single person at the park could be

hiding a terrible secret. Suspicion and unease tingled over her skin.

"Cold?" Declan asked, slinging his arm around her and drawing her closer.

Was it her imagination, or had he grown warmer since he'd turned? And it wasn't just his body heat that had changed. He was bigger and more solid. Strength radiated from him. But the changes weren't only physical. It seemed that he read her more easily, picked up on her emotions. She thought about something she'd learned from her dog, Wordsworth. All emotions have a smell. She shifted away from Declan, a little uneasy that he could interpret her better than she could understand him. It made them an uneven pair—like a plow horse yoked to a colt. She shivered and wrapped her arms around her knees.

Declan ran his fingers through her hair. "As long as we're together, I don't care where we are. You're better than any pack."

"Lots of...I was going to say people, but that doesn't seem like the right word."

"Paranormals?"

She nodded. "Lots of paranormals would argue with you."

"Probably, but who needs them?"

"I think you do. We all need a tribe."

"So says the girl raised on a deserted island."

She grinned. "Thanks for making my point. Living alone with my mom on the island wasn't healthy."

"And you think staying here and being a target for Godwin is?"

"We don't know if you're a target... He hasn't tried anything since—"

"My mom's accident?"

"Well, there was that..."

"He's probably just lying low until the right time."

"He must know that you've turned."

Declan nodded.

Lizbet leaned against his shoulder and lifted her lips so he could kiss her. "I'd go anywhere with you, but we should learn everything we can about being a werewolf." A thought fluttered through her. "Let's go and talk to Dr. Madison."

"He's going to think I'm crazy," Declan said. "Do you think he'll talk to me?"

"Of course he would. Why wouldn't he?"

"Will you ask him after your next class?"

Semester is over, remember? So, why don't you come with me to his office?"

"What, now?"

"Why not?"

Lizbet tucked her hand around Declan's arm. It was a friendly gesture, but also a way to make sure he didn't bolt. She glanced down the empty hall. Since classes didn't

start again for another few days, they really didn't have any guarantee that Dr. Madison would be in. But she didn't know where else to turn. She jumped to her feet when she spotted the professor ambling toward them.

He didn't seem surprised to see them and his words confirmed Lizbet's hunch. "I know why you're here," he said as he unlocked his office door.

Declan shot Lizbet a questioning glance and she responded with a shrug.

Dr. Madison held the door open and motioned for them to take a seat in the two chairs facing his desk. He rested his butt against his desk and studied Declan. "After all, it's not every day a new wolf is born. And of course, losing a pack member is always a tragedy. Leo..." He hung his head.

Lizbet and Declan both stared at him. Lizbet's mouth hung open so long the back of her throat began to grow dry.

Dr. Madison removed his glasses and cleaned them with a small white cloth. "Of course, I can't blame you," he addressed Lizbet. "You were only trying to protect yourself...and those you love."

"The sheep... He was a monster..." Lizbet sputtered.

"Some call us that, yes."

"You?" Declan could barely get the word out. "You're telling us that you're a werewolf too?"

"Of course you can't tell anyone. But your silence is assured by your own state of affairs, is it not?" He went around his desk, settled into his chair, and gazed at them

as calmly as if they were talking about the weather. His eyes crinkled with kindness. "This is not what you were expecting. I understand that. It was different for me, but not so very different."

"How so?" Declan gasped.

Lizbet heard the despair in his voice and reached over and took his hand.

"Well, I wasn't turned as you were. My father, brothers, and uncles are all cursed... Cursed. It's the term we use, but it's not really so bad."

Declan swallowed audibly. "How can you say that?"

"There's an upside to everything. You may have noticed an increase in strength and speed, and your senses will heighten."

"But for three nights of every month I turn into a monster."

"Only if you choose."

Declan leaned back in his chair. "So it's true? I don't have to be a werewolf?"

Dr. Madison placed his elbows on his desk. "There's always a choice. You can learn to control the monster, or you can let the monster control you. You decide."

Lizbet grinned as relief swept through her. She elbowed Declan. "That's what we were saying."

Declan grinned. "This is really good news."

"But you will always be a werewolf."

"But you just said—"

"Pretending otherwise would be a mistake. You must

learn to subdue the creature and yet still honor it." He smiled. "It's much more difficult than you might think."

"Tonight—" Declan began.

"Yes, the first night of the full moon. Meet me in the woods beyond the town green. Do you know where I mean?"

Declan nodded.

Dr. Madison turned to Lizbet. "You may come, if you choose, but tell no one else."

"And you'll teach Declan how to not be a monster?"

"Yes. Although he will always be a werewolf—he needn't be a monster." He chuckled. "It's all semantics, is it not? 'Monster' has a different definition for everyone."

Declan and Lizbet stood at the edge of the woods bordering the town green. The sun had melted into the mountains and the promise of a moon glimmered in a dusky sky. Declan's skin tingled with nerves and dread.

"You can control this," Lizbet said.

"Do you trust him? I'm not sure I completely trust him..."

"Why would he lie?"

Declan glanced over the town green's long stretch of lawn and peered into the shadowy woods. "Why isn't he here?"

"He'll be here."

He squeezed her hand. "You should go."

"Huh-uh." Lizbet shook her head and tightened her grip on Declan's hand. "I'm not leaving."

Declan tilted his head and gazed at the almost-there moon. "I could change any moment. I don't want you to get hurt."

"You wouldn't hurt me."

He lifted an eyebrow. "I wouldn't want to...but I don't trust myself."

"I trust you."

"You shouldn't." His thoughts went back to the conversation he'd heard on the wind. From his readings, he'd learned that pack members could read the thoughts of each other. That's why he'd been privy to those half-whispers. A chill passed over him when he remembered that they meant Lizbet harm. "You have to go," he said much more forcibly.

"No! I'm not leaving you with a pack of wild animals."

"You like animals."

"Of course I do, but—"

Declan interrupted her. "Here comes Dr. Madison. Please go home."

She shuffled her feet. "I don't feel good about this."

He bent and gave her a quick kiss. "Go!" He watched her walk away before turning his attention to the professor striding across the green.

"Where is she going?" Dr. Madison asked after they greeted each other.

"I thought she'd be safer away from here."

Dr. Madison chuckled. "Maybe so. Maybe so." He clapped his hands and rubbed them together. "Ready to get started?"

"I suppose."

"Good!" He motioned toward the woods. "After you, my boy."

They walked a few paces in silence. The trees shivered in a slight breeze. Declan glanced around at the dark shadows, searching for the animals Lizbet counted as friends. He didn't see any and he paused to wonder about that.

"Coming?" Dr. Madison asked without turning around.

Declan wondered about that, too, before remembering that as a werewolf, he, and he presumed the professor, had heightened senses.

As the darkness deepened, Declan's tingling sensation increased. His heartrate picked up speed. "Professor?"

Declan stopped and stared at the hair on his arms growing thicker.

"Ah, yes, it's beginning." Dr. Madison stopped in front of him. "Don't try to fight it. That never works."

"I thought you said I have a choice." Declan watched as the buttons popped off his shirt as his chest expanded.

"You do." Dr. Madison waved at Declan. "You should probably just remove your pants before—"

The snap on Declan's jeans flew into the night. Declan scrambled out of his pants. His own claws scratched his skin. He stared in horror at his furry thighs.

"You said I had a choice!" Declan yelled.

"You do. Here, watch." Dr. Madison pointed at himself. "Now I am a man." He turned his back on Declan

and calmly removed his clothes before transforming into a wolf. He turned back. "And now I'm a wolf."

He spoke, but he didn't use his mouth. The communication was instantaneous but didn't require vocal cords or even ears. It was as if Dr. Madison spoke directly into Declan's mind. As Declan puzzled over this, he became aware of other conversations buzzing around him.

The girl!

Don't let her go!

Declan screamed Lizbet's name, but his voice turned into a long, shuddering howl.

In the Victorian fairy tale, the female's role is merely passive. She is to sit and wait upon her tuffet, languish in a tower with nothing more taxing to do than grow her hair, or spin hay into gold—ever waiting upon her hero who will deliver her to her happily ever after.
From Lizbet's Studies

Chapter 14

Lizbet stared in horror at the circle of green-eyed wolves surrounding her. Two more dashed from the woods. One of them, she felt sure, had to be Declan. The leaner one sprang to her side. "Declan?" she whispered. "Is that you?"

The wolves began to yip and howl as they crouched before her in pounce-position.

"Lizbet! Over here!" Nicole stood in a clearing, pale and as substantial as a blade of grass in the wind. Her blond hair shimmered in the moonlight.

Lizbet studied the wolves. They snarled beneath her gaze.

Nicole waved at her.

Lizbet took a tentative step and the wolves did nothing to stop her. Squaring her shoulders, she headed for Nicole. The wolves in unspoken agreement fell into a single-file line behind her.

"Declan." Lizbet said his name in a rush. "I can't find him."

Nicole grabbed her hand. "I'll bring him to you."

The wolves' breath fanned the back of Lizbet's legs. She shivered more from fright than cold.

"Come on." Nicole tugged on her hand.

"Where are we going?" Lizbet stumbled beside her.

"Somewhere safe," Nicole said, pulling her forward.

"But Declan... He has to be here. He must be one of those animals..." A realization hit her and she froze. "You're one, too."

"Not anymore," Nicole said.

Lizbet gazed up at the full moon. "Then it's true. You don't have to be a werewolf?"

"Some people can control it, yes."

"And you can?"

Nicole rolled her eyes. "Well, obviously. Now, come on! My family has a cabin just through the woods. You'll be safe there."

Just as Lizbet had noticed before, as long as the wolves were around, all the other animals were scarce. A few owls flew overhead, but they didn't get close enough to talk to. Lizbet had so many questions niggling in the back of her mind and the only person there to answer them was Nicole.

And she didn't trust Nicole—but if she had to choose between Nicole and the wolves, she'd pick Nicole. Unless one of the creatures was Declan, as she suspected. But she had no idea which one he was...or if he was even there. She thought he was. She liked to think she could sense him, but...she didn't trust her senses, either. So, she

tripped along the path, letting Nicole pull her deeper into the woods.

The wind whipped through the trees. Branches swayed, creaking their complaints of the brewing storm. Declan sprang after Lizbet and Nicole, but the pack formed a furry, snarling wall. He wanted to fight them all, but he knew if he tried, he would die.

A large black wolf stepped out of the pack. The fur on his scruff pointed to the cloud-shrouded moon. His eyes were a terrible green.

Godwin.

You recognize me in my native form. I'm glad. Now you'll know it's me when I kill you.

At this pronouncement, the wolves' collective growls grew deeper and hungrier. Declan braced for the attack he knew would come.

But not quite yet. A little torture is in order. I want you to watch the pretty girl die first.

You can't kill Lizbet. She's protected by the animals.

Godwin's eyes flickered with amusement. *Do you see any of her woodland friends?*

Declan glanced around the forest. Other than the gathered wolves, it was still and silent. *What did you do to them?*

Nothing...other than terrorize them. Even the bears are wise enough to give the pack a wide berth.

Still, Lizbet is special—

So thinks every smitten puppy. It's useful, this obsession of yours. It guarantees your death.

How so?

Well, there is a law...a pesky regulation. Pack members aren't allowed to kill each other, unless one is a traitor to the pack.

I'm not a member of your pack.

Oh, but you are. You turned because of us. That makes you one of us...unless...

Unless what?

You renounce the pack. You see, as a pack member you must swear total allegiance to the pack. Our safety must be your first concern. It's the only way we can survive. But you—why I believe you'll choose the girl over your brothers. Drool fell from his lips. *For this treason, I can kill you. But first, I must hear you say it.*

Godwin jerked his furry head in the direction Lizbet and Nicole had disappeared. Surrounded as he was by the pack, Declan had no other choice but to follow. Not that he would have taken a different path. Because Godwin was right. He would always choose the girl. Even over himself.

He followed the wolves over a hill and around a bend to a small clearing. Clouds shifted and a shaft of moonlight landed on a small cabin. Declan watched through the window as Nicole bolted the cabin door.

"We'll be safe in here," Nicole told Lizbet.

Godwin chuckled. *Ironic, isn't it? Her thinking she's safe. As long as you live, she'll never be safe.*

Lizbet shivered as a realization swept through her. She'd rather take her chances with Declan and the wolves than with Nicole. "I made a mistake in coming here," she told Nicole as she headed for the door.

Nicole sprang forward, snarling, and phasing into a wolf. Lizbet unbolted the door and threw it open. Nicole hit the door's edge and fell to the floor with a yelp.

A large gray wolf jumped to her side. Could he be Declan in creature form? She didn't know, couldn't be sure, until he leaned against her and the familiar rush of warmth Declan's touch always evoked ran through her.

As Declan pressed his furry side against her leg. Lizbet's thoughts raced. These animals meant her harm, but why? And was it her? Or was it Declan that they wanted? Would she just be collateral damage? Or could she save herself and Declan as well?

Not seeing any animals, other than the snarling ones before her, Lizbet heard Mawmaw's words come back to her. *"All nature—plants, weather, the moon and stars."*

She summoned the wind. *Come to me,* she breathed. It answered with a rush of warm air. Bolstered by this small success, she raised her arms above her head.

"Lightning! Thunder of the sky,
Send your magic nigh,
Wind, fan the flames,
Show the world where true power reigns!"

A lightning bolt shot through the sky, thunder boomed, and clouds that appeared from nowhere poured rain. Lizbet smiled as memories flooded through her. She saw her mother, remembered their time together, and the lessons she'd learned as a child came rushing back even as the largest black wolf sprang at her.

Lizbet gathered her energy and directed a lightning bolt at the wolf's head. He skittered sideways while his pack scattered. Lightning struck the tree with a deafening crack. Sparks lit the air like a hundred lethal fireflies.

The black wolf lunged at her, but the gray wolf at her side went for his neck. The wolves rose to their back legs, pawing each other and snarling.

Lizbet picked up a burning fallen branch and jabbed it in the face of the black wolf. He yipped as the fire singed his fur. Still, he leapt toward Lizbet. She stumbled back, holding the burning branch aloft. Summoning another bolt of lightning, she landed on her back and her head hit the ground with a solid smack. Darkness overcame her.

Sirens wailed.

The pack's unspoken words swirled around Declan.

Men.

Fire.

The girl. She killed the alpha. Kill the girl.

Declan stood guard, ready to fight should any of the pack decide to brave the fire surrounding Lizbet.

The sirens stopped at the edge of the woods. *Voices. Men.*

Declan glanced at Lizbet. She lay in a circle of flames. Godwin, the man, lay naked beside her.

The men would find her soon. She would be safe. For the moment. But as long as she was with Declan, she'd never really be safe again. Her only shot at a long, happy life was without him. Away from the forest. Surrounded by people who lived by a higher code than wolves...and paranormals. His disappearance wouldn't only protect Lizbet, but also his mom and his dad...his friends. Everyone he loved would be safer if he wasn't around.

He tore himself away. Somewhere in the west, the ocean called. He heard it above the wind, beyond the call of gulls. He'd follow the coast north. He would go where no one could ever find him.

Hunger tore through him. He zigzagged through the forest in search of food. A light shone through the trees. He turned off the main road, followed a dirt road down the bank and stopped in front of a moss-colored wood-frame house. A duck's stripped carcass hung from the porch eaves. He leaped up, ripped it from its tether, and chewed on its flesh and bones.

The door banged open and a small wizened woman emerged from the house. She wore a large flannel shirt, a baggy pair of jeans, and a bandana wrapped around her gray-streaked dark hair. She eyed him warily before placing a bowl of water in front of him. After inhaling the duck, he drank.

Chapter 15

Her eyelids felt heavy, as if weighted, and yet unsubstantial against the unnatural white glare. She licked her lips; they were cracked, dry, and tasted of blood and ash. Her head pounded. Someone touched her hand and whispered what sounded like an apology. "Lizbet?"

"Mom?" Her eyes flickered open and her mother's face swam into focus. Immediately, she began to cry hot tears that made her cheeks sting. She remembered falling into the flames. There had been horrific pain and then nothing. "Where's Declan?" she asked.

"Oh, baby," her mom said, and her voice cracked. She pressed Lizbet against her in a fierce hug, but when Lizbet winced in pain she gently let go and settled her against the pillows. Lizbet took note of Daugherty's tired, lined face, the gray sprinkling in her hair, and her worried blue eyes.

Lizbet slipped a hand into her mom's and looked beyond her to the sterile white hospital walls. Outside, the distant lights of Queen Anne Boulevard sparkled in the twilight. Cars rushed up and down the parkway; street signals flashed yellow, green and red; a blinking airplane headed for the airport. Courtney and Malcolm were probably in Alaska by now. But where was Declan?

She touched her head where it was tender and felt the bump beneath her fingers. She understood the pain, but that didn't explain everything.

Not at all.

"Is Declan...?" She couldn't say the word.

A sob came from the other side of the bed. Elizabeth, red-eyed, sunken-cheeked, gray and worn.

Lizbet let her heavy eyelids close, trying to make sense of her new world. A world without Declan.

A battery of tests and visits from doctors filled the next day. During the poking, prodding, and bandage-changing Lizbet learned a few things: a lightning strike had sparked a forest fire. The remains of eight people—all charred beyond recognition—had been recovered. Declan, along with Nicole Gunner, was believed to be among the dead. Lizbet had been found beneath a tangle of the scorched trees. No one could explain how she'd survived. She'd been in the hospital, unconscious, for four days.

Lizbet closed her eyes against all this information. She tried to process the hospital truth with the myths of the Ollos Verdes, werewolves, and vampires. But while her mind told her one thing, her heart said something else entirely.

"It's common for a patient suffering severe physical and emotional distress to have delusional episodes," Dr. Meehan, a mental health counselor, told her. "It's your mind trying to escape the horror of your reality." The doctor, a petite blond in an oversized lab coat, had purple-polka-dot nail polish. She looked a lot like Courtney.

It hurt to talk through cracked lips with a dry and scratchy throat, so Lizbet didn't try. Worrying that she'd lost her mind was making her crazy.

Dr. Meehan shifted in the chair beside the bed and settled a clipboard in her lap. "There's a great deal of research and controversy concerning the workings of our subconscious. Some say dreams are a random firing of neurons and have no meaning. Spiritualists believe they are messages from God."

"It seemed so real," Lizbet muttered, staring past the doctor and out the window, beyond the bustling city to the green hills where the canyon began. "And there are so many things I didn't know, that I couldn't have imagined... like the Ollos Verdes."

Dr. Meehan smiled. "Our subconscious minds are incredibly powerful. We know many things that we've never given much thought to, yet our brains have filed away the information." She patted Lizbet's hand. "You

can't believe the nightmare. You can't argue with it, or challenge it. Your only option is to destroy it."

"Destroy it?" Lizbet thought of Declan, his face, his smile. How could she destroy the memories of someone she loved? But maybe that was exactly what she had done.

Dr. Meehan gave her a kind and sympathetic look. "It's not real, so it can't be destroyed literally. The only way to defuse its power is to shine your light of reason upon it. There's no other option. You can't believe the lie, but you might find it helpful to write it down. It will help you clarify your feelings. Journaling about such a traumatic experience will let you explore, process and release your emotions."

The doctor gathered her things and rose to her feet. "You're lucky that you have so many people who love you. If you're interested in journaling, I'll get you a pad of paper and a pen."

"Thank you," Lizbet lisped, wetting her lips and tasting ash. "I'd like that."

Dr. Meehan patted Lizbet's hand again before leaving.

Pushing herself up on the bed, Lizbet saw her reflection in the window. With her singed hair, chapped red skin, and swollen lips, she looked like someone else. She was ugly, inside and out. She had killed Declan as surely as if she'd put a gun to his head, pulled the trigger, and sent a bullet into his brain.

Three weeks later, Lizbet sat at the table with her grandmother and toyed with the slice of cake in front of her with a fork. This was supposed to be a celebration and a homecoming, but Lizbet knew she'd never be able to celebrate again.

"I don't like it one little bit," Elizabeth groused.

"We've been over this, Grandma. There's nothing you can do to stop me." Lizbet pushed cake crumbs across her plate.

"In my day, young girls didn't just hike off into the hinder-parts on their own."

Lizbet sighed. "I'm not going alone. Matias and Maria are coming with me to the tribe of Stehekin. It's only for a few days."

"I just don't understand why they don't have roads. They must not want visitors if they don't have roads."

"I agree." Lizbet took a bite of her cake. It tasted like sawdust.

Elizabeth gave her a squinty-eyed look. "Why do you want to visit someone who doesn't want visitors?"

"I'm curious. They're my people."

"No. I'm your people. Your mom is your people. Love is always thicker than blood."

"I love you, too, Grandma. But the Stehekin tribe is my heritage. I want to learn all I can about them."

"You might not like what you learn."

Lizbet put down her fork so she could pat her grandmother's hand. "I'll be fine. I'll be back before school starts. You won't even miss me."

Even though it was mid-September and the rest of the Western Hemisphere was at the end of summer, in the high Cascades, the leaves were already turning to shades of red, orange, and yellow. Sitting on Trotter's back on the mountain peak, Lizbet could see for miles. Far below them in the Methow Valley, a fire burned. It promised disaster for those who lived in the thick of it, but from this great distance, the smoke cloud looked as threatening as a cotton boll. Still, the thought of a forest fire turned Lizbet's stomach and she wondered if she'd ever be able to be near open flames again without having a panic attack.

Trotter must have sensed her unease, because he balked on the trail.

Matias looked over his shoulder at her. "You okay?"

She nodded and rubbed a hand over Trotter's sleek neck. "Do you think the horses need water?"

Maria pulled alongside her. "I think I hear a stream. Let me check the map."

A cardinal flying overhead pointed his wing to the left. *"Not far!"* he called.

Lizbet urged Trotter off the path. "It's this way."

"I don't know how you do this," Maria muttered. "You're like a divining rod."

"I just have good hearing," Lizbet joked as she led Trotter through the tall grass to a thicket of birch trees.

Maria and Matias followed close behind on their horses. The nearer they drew to the water, the more audible the stream became. Lizbet said a silent thanks to the cardinal as he flitted overhead.

Once they reached the creek's bank, she slipped off Trotter to let him drink. Maria did the same, and rummaged through her saddlebag looking for the guide book.

Matias found a giant fallen log and rested his butt against it.

"We should be close," Maria said, studying the guide.

"It's hard to believe people still actually live like this," Matias said.

"The Stehckin aren't the only ones," Maria said. "There are tribes living at the bottom of the Grand Canyon. Their only access to the outside world is a ten-mile donkey trail or a two-minute helicopter ride."

"We could have taken a helicopter?" Matias asked in a wounded tone.

"This is more fun," Lizbet said.

Matias rubbed his back with both hands. "For who?"

Lizbet laughed and pulled a roll of toilet paper and a trowel from her bag. "Don't follow me!" She followed the stream until she reached a cluster of boulders that could provide shelter and privacy.

A small dark-haired and green-eyed woman stepped out of the trees. She carried a pipe in her right hand.

Lizbet's heart jumped. "You scared me!"

"As I should," the woman said, right before she put the pipe in her mouth and blew a puff of smoke in Lizbet's face.

The world went dark.

Lifting one eyelid, Lizbet took note of a few dim stars twinkling in the darkening sky. She crawled out from beneath a heavy wool blanket to peek out the door. A circular fence made of poles shoved into the ground encompassed the village. About thirty round huts filled the enclosure, and one large pavilion-like building stood in the center. Smoke filled the pavilion. A large woman with ebony skin and grizzled gray hair dressed in batik cloth stood at the foot of an altar with her arms raised to the sky, her face also turned heavenward. Men, women, and children gathered around her. The sound of beating drums and chanting filled the air. Lizbet scooted so that her back pressed against the wall. *How had she gotten to this place?*

"The question is simple. It's the answer that most find difficult." A man's voice answered her unspoken question.

Lizbet swiveled her attention to a small man with leathery skin, graying dark hair, and eyes the color of her own. He sat cross-legged on a mat in the corner. She wondered how long he had been there, apparently doing nothing more than watching her sleep.

"Who are you?" Lizbet gasped, afraid that she already knew the answer.

"You know who I am."

She swallowed down a lump of anger. "Where have you been all of my life?"

"Have you been unhappy with Daugherty?"

"I could have used you!"

"What use would I have been in the world of men?" He waited for her answer, but she didn't have one.

"You left me an orphan!"

"Is that how you see yourself?"

Lizbet thought of her mother, Elizabeth, and even cranky Josie. "Not really...but I always wanted a father. Everyone does."

"But did you want a father like me?"

"How can I answer that? I don't even know you."

"And now you have the chance...and the choice."

"The choice of what?"

"Will you choose the life of men, or the ways of the Ollos Verdes?"

"Why can't I have both?"

He sighed. "This, I'm afraid, is the path your mother chose. It is the way of heartbreak. If you choose to live in touch with nature—as you have up to this point—you must devote yourself wholly to its pleasure."

"What does that even mean?" Lizbet rubbed her aching head.

"Your mother had been unable to decide between devotion to Mother Earth and a life with a man. She lived a half-life—neither here nor there. She tried to find a balance between the two. And it killed her."

"That's not what killed her. Godwin—a werewolf—killed her."

He nodded. "Yes. The wolves hate the Ollos Verdes. That's why we must stay together."

"So, what you're saying is if I want to be able to control the weather, I need to sequester myself away from the world and devote the rest of my life to safeguarding the earth?"

"You do more than control the weather."

Lizbet struggled to sit up, but a gentle hand pressed her back down against the mat. "Wait. What are you saying?"

"Your communion with the animals. This will also be lost."

"But..." She tried to imagine a world where she could no longer talk to animals. "I could talk to them?"

Her father nodded. "And they will talk to you."

"Then there's no problem."

"Except you will not understand them."

Realization dawned. "I'll be like everyone else."

"Everyone except for the Ollos Verdes."

"And to be a part of the Ollos Verdes I need to live here...in seclusion."

His lips twitched. "It's not so bad. You will, I believe, enjoy it."

"But why not be a part of the rest of the world?"

He shook his head. "You will find it too painful. Mother Earth is a demanding mistress."

"But what good can we do here? Don't we have to be in the world if we want to change the world?"

Her father smiled in response, but still looked sad. "You would like to try, wouldn't you?"

"Yes, I would. I'm not willing to give up my relationships with my mom, my grandmother, and my friends..." Lizbet lay on her back staring up at a star-studded sky. "And how can I not know what I already know?"

"The gift will still be inside you, but you will forget it's there, so you will no longer reach for it. It's like a tool that you will have forgotten you possess."

"I still don't understand."

"Without the protection of the tribe, you will never survive as an Ollos Verdes in the world of men."

Lizbet thrust out her chin. She didn't fear anyone. She'd faced the wolves and won...or had she? She'd lost Declan. The pain of his loss swept through her. She couldn't lose her mom and grandmother as well.

He slowly nodded. "I see you've made your decision. Before you go, will you not join me in a glass of wine?"

When Lizbet hesitated, he added, "I think you'll find it to be the tonic you need."

He held a glass filled with amber liquid in front of him.

And Lizbet, thinking of Mawmaw's wine, drank.

Lizbet woke to find Maria and Matias stretched out side by side on a blanket, asleep. She sat up, braced her elbows on her knees, and cradled her aching head. "Such a strange dream," she muttered to no one.

Pulling herself up, she leaned against Trotter while she rummaged through her saddlebag in search of the first aid kit and a bottle of aspirin.

Trotter blew out a warm breath and nuzzled her hair.

"I love you, too," she said, patting him.

He snorted and neighed in response, and she found an apple and held it while he munched on it. She looked up at the moon hovering above the trees. "I guess this is as good a place as any to camp for the night." But why had they fallen asleep before setting up the tent or starting a fire? Had they eaten dinner? She couldn't remember anything but the strange dream and the man claiming to be her father.

While her friends slept, Lizbet pitched the tent. That night she had crazy dreams of talking animals and werewolves.

They spent the next three days wandering beneath the hot August sun.

"I don't get it," Matias groused. "For two days it was like you had an inner honing device—and now we're walking in circles."

Lizbet laughed. "I didn't really get us anywhere, you know." She looked up at the sky. A flock of geese flew in

a perfect V formation on their way to warmer climates. The birds were headed south and the humans would be wise to follow.

"I guess the Ollos Verdes Indians was really just a legend after all," Maria said.

"Home is that way," Lizbet said, using the geese as her compass.

Matias shrugged. "Ready to give up?"

"I guess... It was fun. I don't know what made me think I could find something others have been searching for eons."

"Optimism," Matias said grimly, but with a hidden smile. "It's been making people do crazy things for years."

Chapter 16

Declan froze.

It had been a common enough experience in the past ten years since he'd disappeared from his life in Washington and reinvented himself in Alaska, but this freezing had nothing to do with the temperature—still brisk, even in September, one of Anchorage's more pleasant months—and everything to do with his heart.

Lizbet. Had she followed him? After all this time? She stood on the sidewalk in front of a display of wildflowers, touching the leaves of a basil plant. His memory flashed back to their time at the nursery, when she and old Mr. Neal would sing to the plants. Declan had teased her for it, saying that plants couldn't hear her—that was before he knew she could not only sing to them, but persuade them to do whatever she asked.

She must have felt his gaze, because she lifted her eyes to meet his. He waited for a flash of recognition, but saw nothing more than warm curiosity. He flinched as if she'd struck him and turned away.

Shoving his hands into his pockets, he headed home. When he was sure she couldn't hear him, he pulled his phone out of his pocket and called Malcolm.

"Lizbet's here," he said without preamble.

"Are you sure?"

"Absolutely."

"It's been ten years, dude."

"I know." Declan raked his fingers through his hair.

"How long was your last rotation?"

"Does that matter?"

Malcolm borrowed Declan's word. "Absolutely. How much sleep have you gotten in the last forty-eight hours?"

"Almost none, but that doesn't matter. What matters is that LIZBET IS HERE."

"Okay, calm down. Let me see..." Declan heard the tap of Malcolm's fingers on a keyboard. Since his arrival in Anchorage, Malcolm had not only married Courtney, but he'd started a tech company that helped paranormals connect their business needs, and also protected their privacy.

Declan sat down on a bench in Delany Park and watched a young kid throw a ball for a golden retriever. Memories of his dog Rufus flooded him. Declan battled to control his emotions.

"Lizbet, as you know," Malcolm said, "has a PhD from the University of Washington in English Literature and she specializes in folklore...huh...interesting. I guess you're right."

"What? Tell me."

"She's on sabbatical and will be teaching at the University of Anchorage."

Declan pulled on his hair. "What am I going to do?"

"What do you want to do?"

"I don't know..."

Malcolm cleared his throat. "Maybe you should talk to Courtney. She's better at this sort of thing."

"I don't want—"

Courtney cut Declan off and took the phone. "Declan, if you're worried about her recognizing you—"

"It's not that, it's just..." His eyes focused on a pair of women's black leather boots. He slowly drew his gaze up to meet Lizbet's. He ended the call and tucked the phone into his pocket.

"Hi," she said, looking uncomfortable. "I thought...for a moment...it's just you remind me of someone I used to know."

He squirmed beneath the intensity of her gaze.

"But..." She shook her head. "Sorry."

"No, it's okay." He scooched over and patted the spot next to him on the bench. "Are you new here?"

She laughed, and his heart ached at the memories the sound bombarded him with.

"Is it so obvious?"

"No, it's just...I think I would have noticed you...had I seen you before." He was having a hard time stringing words together. He'd be lost if she asked him something more complex than his name. And even though he'd been living with his new name for almost a decade, he wasn't a hundred percent sure he'd be able to keep the lie around her.

"I'm Lizbet Wood," she said, sticking out her hand.

"John Hart." He took her hand. She still gave him tingles.

"John. That's my stepfather's name. It's also the name of the father of the boy I'd mistaken you for." Slowly, she pulled her hand from his and tucked it in her coat pocket.

"Strange coincidence."

She cocked her head to stare at him. "Really? Do you think so?"

He shrugged and tried to look innocent. "Do you believe in coincidences?"

"Yeah."

"Some people don't."

She flipped her hair over her shoulder—something he'd seen her do a hundred times. The movement sent a breath of air carrying her own unique scent into his face. He recoiled as if she'd struck him.

"But I do," she said. "I don't think everything has to happen for a reason."

He swallowed hard, trying to rein in his emotions. "You don't believe in fate or kismet?"

"Not really."

"What brings you to Alaska, Ms. Wood?"

"I'm a literature professor. I'm going to teach a few classes at the University." She pointed her chin in the school's direction. "And I'm going to be recording local lore from the Native Americans in the region."

"Huh. You sound awfully skeptical for a teacher of fairy tales."

She toyed with a loose string on her sweater. "My faith in happily-ever-afters took a beating. Went up in flames, actually."

"How so?"

"Oh, I... It's too soon to talk about it."

"Too soon?"

"Well, the fire was actually more than a decade ago. What I meant was, we just met. You don't want to hear my sad story, do you?"

"We all have sad stories."

"True, but we don't have to tell them. I guess that's why I like fairy tales."

"Because they always have a happily-ever-after?"

She nodded.

A blue jay landed on the back of the bench and Lizbet flinched away. Strange.

"You don't like birds?" Declan asked.

"I like to look at them, and listen to them, especially in the morning." She wrinkled her nose. "But I think they're dirty and disgusting creatures."

Declan sat up. "Aren't you worried he'll hear you?"

"Who? The bird?" She laughed.

A small frisson of worry tickled down Declan's spine. He didn't know this Lizbet. She was the same, but different. What had happened to her in the past ten years?

"I'd like to introduce you to my dog. Do you like dogs?" he asked.

"Sure."

He studied her. She was beautiful, of course, but different. More poised. Stiller. Less distracted. "You don't sound sure."

"I actually prefer cats."

He chuckled and leaned back against the bench. He wanted to relax, but his mind whirred with questions. "Well, let's not tell that to Stoker."

"Stoker? Like Bram Stoker, the creator of Dracula?"

"Actually, I'm pretty sure Stoker didn't create Dracula." He pushed his hand through his hair. "He just wrote about him."

"What do you do?" She cocked her head at him.

"I'm a doctor, as well...only my work is bloodier."

An emotion he couldn't read flickered across her face. "The boy I lost in the fire, he wanted to be a doctor, too."

"I'm sorry."

She ducked her head. "Me, too."

"But remember, it's too soon for sad stories."

"You're right." She sighed. "Your work must be really something if you think you can out-bloody Dracula."

"I'm a surgeon, so I see a fair amount of blood." He paused. "Do you study vampires?"

"And werewolves...all monsters, really."

"But you...don't believe in them, do you?"

"Do you?"

"You're dodging my question."

"Actually, it's called a counter-question."

"What is?"

"When you answer a question with a question." She looked at her watch and let out a sigh. "I have to go."

Panic clutched Declan's throat, making it hard to swallow or breathe. He couldn't let her go. Again. "I was serious about introducing you to Stoker."

She smiled and fished in her pocket for her card and a pen. "I'm teaching a class tonight on mythical creatures. Would you like to attend? I'd invite Stoker, too, but sadly only service dogs are allowed on campus."

"I'd love to."

She hid her smile behind a curtain of her curly hair as she wrote down the place and time of her lecture on the back of her card.

"Here," she said.

He glanced at the card. Beneath her name was the caption, *Fairy tales can come true.*

This was something he hadn't believed until she reappeared in his life.

Declan woke, shivering despite the quilt thrown over him. The sun was still little more than a pinkish smear on the eastern horizon. He braced himself on his elbows and looked out at the forest surrounding the wooden porch. His feet dangled over the edge and a large and ugly dog softly snored beside him.

"What happened?" he asked the inert dog. Sitting up, he realized he was naked.

"What did you see?" a voice asked.

Mawmaw, Matias and Maria's grandmother, the woman who brewed the crazy wine. What was she doing here? He took in his surroundings—the weather-beaten house, the scraggly lawn, the aged dog, and altered his question. "What am I doing here?"

She rocked her chair back and studied him. "You came by last night, in wolf form. I fed you."

"Thank you."

Her grin deepened. "You're welcome."

He scratched his unshaven chin. "I don't know what's real and what's not."

"You aren't the only one, I'm sure."

"I'm still a werewolf."

She nodded. "And you always will be."

"But I can learn to control it."

"For the girl's sake, I hope you do."

A haze that smelled like a campfire hung in the air.

"There was a fire last night," he said. *Was it just last night?*

She nodded.

"And—"

"Many of the wolves died. The others fled."

His heart quickened. "And Lizbet?"

"She's home with her mother and grandmother."

Declan stood. Too late, he remembered he was naked. Embarrassed, he grabbed at the quilt.

Mawmaw just smiled. "My husband has some clothes you can borrow. Stay there, and I'll fetch them for you."

Declan dropped back to his seat on the porch. By the time Mawmaw returned with a pair of jeans and a flannel shirt, he'd gathered his wits enough to ask a few questions.

"The dream... it was all a dream, wasn't it? Lizbet meeting her father and losing her abilities...Does it have to come true?"

"Only if you want it to." She eyed him. "We might not have the power to alter our destinies, but we all can steer in the direction we wish to go."

Declan nodded. "And Lizbet living as an Ollos Verde—does she have to live with the tribe?"

"I can't really answer that. Only she can...in time. But I will tell you that we all need a tribe. No man can survive on his own."

Mawmaw gestured toward the house. "You can change in privacy." He knew she was talking about the clothes, but the words held an invitation for so much more.

Lizbet flew down the stairs when she heard Declan's voice. Launching herself into his arms, she buried her face in his shoulder. "I was so scared! Where did you go?"

He swung her around before kissing her.

Elizabeth, who stood in the foyer, cleared her throat.

Lizbet ignored her grandmother, but Declan whispered in Lizbet's ear, "Let's go outside."

As soon as they stepped out onto the front porch, Lizbet pulled away and smacked his arm. "What happened to you last night?"

"As soon I knew you were safe, I was going to run away... In fact, I thought I had."

"What?"

Taking her hand, he led her down the porch steps, away from the house and any open windows. Once they were out of earshot from anyone other than birds and the goats in the field, Declan wrapped his arm around her shoulder. "My plan was to go to Alaska with Malcolm and Courtney. But...Matias and Maria's mawmaw stopped me. She gave me some of that crazy-making wine." He stopped at the fence and crawled through.

She followed.

"I had a vision," he continued. "And in it, you met the other Ollos Verdes including your father. He told you that you could either join them in their community, or you could join the rest of us and give up your abilities."

"Which did I choose?"

They walked along the wooded path. Although it was only the end of August, a few of the trees had already started to turn from green to red, gold, and brown.

"You lost your abilities."

She nodded. "I would give them up if that was the only way I could stay with you."

He squeezed her hand. "I would never ask you to change. I only hope you can be patient with me as I learn how to balance being part man and part wolf."

"Dr. Madison was right?"

Declan nodded. "I can control it...somewhat. I guess I have a lifetime to practice. Will you help me?"

"Will you help me?" Lizbet asked.

"You are incredible!" Declan stared up at the sky where a few dark clouds gathered. "Why would you ever want to be anything other than what you are?"

"I caused a fire." She choked on tears. "People died. I couldn't stop it. It's scary."

"Of course it is, but don't you see? The alternative is so much worse."

"To be like everyone else?"

"No, you could never be like anyone else."

She bumped him with her shoulder. "And neither could you."

A few raindrops fell.

Declan cleared his throat. "But do you think you can turn off the waterworks now?"

Lizbet shook her head. "I don't want to. I feel... drained, somehow. I'm not sure I could do it again. At least, not for a while."

"It's a good thing the others have gone."

"Gone? Where? How would you know?"

He explained to her the silent communication amongst the pack. "They're heading to the Canadian Rockies. Ollos Verdes terrify them."

"I'm terrifying." She tried to process this.

"Terrifyingly wonderful," Declan said as he gathered her into his arms and kissed her.

She noticed that they had arrived at the circle of stones.

"This is what Godwin wanted," Declan told her. "The pack had never intended to harm anyone, but they wanted this piece of land. They believe that this place is sacred. The energy here gives them strength."

"Do you believe that?"

He shrugged. "I'm not sure what I believe in anymore. Although there is one thing I know for sure. I don't want to live without you. Ever."

Epilogue

Ten months later

John fussed with his bowtie. "It's lopsided," he muttered.

Declan, who had his own bowtie to worry about, came to help his dad. He tweaked it into shape. "There you go, it looks great."

Declan peeked out of the caterer's tent and scanned the lawn. Dozens of white chairs draped in tulle and lace had been set up in front of a wicker arch decorated with roses and strings of pearls. Friends and family sat waiting. He looked over his dad's shoulder to see his mom sitting beside Holbrook St. James, and Maria sitting with Baxter. The entire school board was there as well as several teachers from the high school. Elizabeth sat in the front row, nervously clutching a string of pearls.

"What if she doesn't show?" John asked.

"Dad, really?"

"Or what if it rains? Who ever heard of an outdoor wedding in the Pacific Northwest?"

Declan grinned. "The weather is, I think, the last thing you should be worried about. I can pretty much guarantee you a life of sunny skies as long as you stay with Daugherty." He glanced at his watch. "It's almost time."

And just then, as if the band had heard him, the violins began to play Mendelssohn's *Wedding March.*

John braced his shoulders and stepped out of the tent. Everyone turned to watch as John proceeded down the aisle and took his place in front of the minister. Declan followed.

Lizbet met him at the aisle and gave him a teary smile along with her hand. When they reached the minister, they broke apart and turned to watch Daugherty make her entrance.

Pale with silvery blond hair, she looked nothing like Lizbet, but as she approached, Declan couldn't help imagining another wedding. His own. To Lizbet. Visions of their future clouded his mind. He saw their graduations from college, a home with white clapboard and blue shutters, a passel of dark curly-haired children and, of course, a menagerie of animals playing in the yard.

I hope you enjoyed reading about Lizbet and Declan. If you did, please consider leaving a review. If you'd like to read more of my books, please go to my website at *http://www.kristytate.com* and sign up for my newsletter to receive a free ebook.

Witch One

By Kristy Tate

Copyright July 2017

When emotions run high, sparks can fly.

How a High School Dance is Like the Courting Rituals Found in the Animal Kingdom
By Evelynn Marston

The animal kingdom is rife with courtship rituals. These are generally initiated by the males who attempt to woo female partners.

Some animals, like the bowerbird, will collect a tower of objects to impress his love. The great grebe, who mates for life, has a series of dance moves to perform throughout the mating season. If, for any reason, the pair is separated, they will each bust a move when reunited. The male peacock spreads his tail feathers and struts around.

The praying mantis literally risks his life for a

night of love. If his lady dislikes his performance, she bites his head off.

A male nursery web spider will present a little bundle of food wrapped in pretty white silk to the female as a request to mate. If the female likes the present, the two will mate while she unwraps and eats the meal. Sadly, sometimes the male will try to bring a wrapped twig. When this happens, the relationship is dead in the water.

It might be thought that courtship only occurs in the kinds of animals that have fairly complex brains, such as mammals and birds. This is not the case as the school dances at Hartly High clearly demonstrate!

Mr. Cox put down my essay and wannabe newspaper article and smiled with a gaze that glittered with excitement. "Are you willing to attend the dance--not as a participant, but as a spectator?"

"Absolutely," I said.

"This is the hallmark of a true journalist," he told me. "You must be able to put aside your own desires. As a reporter, you cease to be an individual with your own petty goals. Your function is to be a communication vessel--a transmitter to the world."

I nodded, mute with happiness.

"You agreed to what?" Bree asked at her house later that night.

I pushed my hair off my forehead and looked across the kitchen table at my best friend. Studying at my own house, where there was no one but Scratch, our bulldog, and the sound of Uncle Mitch's lab rats scurrying in their cages to interrupt us, was quieter and therefore boring compared to hanging at Bree's.

"I'm not going to the dance, per se, as a person." I had expected this conversation and had prepared for it. "I'm going as a journalist."

"So you are going and you can get me a ticket."

"You know only upperclassmen can go."

Lincoln, Bree's little brother, burst into the room wearing nothing but his tighty-whities. "Where are the cookies?" he demanded. His pale skin stretched across his bony chest.

"I don't know anything about cookies," Bree told him. "And go and put your clothes on."

Lincoln scooted a kitchen chair up to the counter for a quick cookie-surveillance and took note of backpacks, textbooks, novels, scribbled-on bits of paper, a baseball card collection. His eyes lit up when he spotted a half-eaten chocolate bunny, probably left over from Easter.

Bree ignored her little brother. "But the Blazing Blizzards!"

"Norfolk High will probably have a great band too."

"That's so not true," Bree said.

"The guys at your school are hotter."

Lincoln stood on his chair and nibbled on one of the bunny's ears.

"What makes you say that?" Bree asked.

"Well, they don't have to wear Hartly's uniform, for one thing."

In the living room, the front door opened and Bree's older sister Candace walked in with a friend wearing a chicken suit. A cold breeze circled the room until the door slammed shut.

"What the quack?" Lincoln asked.

"It's 'what the cluck,'" the girl in the chicken suit corrected him with a giggle.

Candace's friend had masses of blond hair tucked into a hoodie covered with yellow feathers. She wore the beak on top of her head like a rhino horn.

"You look stupid," Lincoln told her.

"Thanks," the girl said.

"What are you supposed to be?"

"I'm a chick," she told him right before she lowered the beak over her nose.

"But why?" Lincoln demanded.

"You'll see," the girl said. The beak bobbed up and down with her muffled words.

"School play try-outs already?" I asked Bree in a hushed tone as soon as the chick and Candace ran up the back stairs.

"I don't think so," Bree said.

"Are the dogs outside?" Candace called from upstairs.

Lincoln jumped off his chair. "Why?" he demanded. "They have just as much right as you do to be in here."

"Just take them out!" Candace called back.

"They're not here," Bree yelled.

"Where are they?"

"I don't know," Bree answered.

"Well, keep them out."

"Why?" Lincoln asked.

The smell of fried chicken wafted down the stairs.

"What the...cluck?" Bree pushed back from the table and went into the front room.

I followed.

Candace and the chick were dropping a trail of chicken nuggets that started at the front door and ran up the stairs.

"Nobody step on these," the chick demanded.

"Does Mom know you're doing this?" Bree asked, her lips curled in disdain.

"She won't care," Candace said as she dropped chicken nuggets on the floor.

"Uncle Mitch would," I said under my breath.

Bree nodded. "I don't think Mom is going to like it, but the dogs will."

"Bree," Candace called. "Come help."

I trailed up the stairs after Bree and followed the nuggets into the bathroom. The chick lay in the bathtub and Candace stood beside her with a roll of plastic wrap in her hands. "We're going to make it look like she's swimming in nuggets."

Bree gawked at the large tinfoil baking pans. "You must have spent a hundred dollars on nuggets!"

"Three hundred and twenty-five dollars," the girl announced from her prone position in the tub.

"But why?" Lincoln pushed into the room.

Candace nodded at the sign hung on the white tile above the tub. It read, "Josh, you'd be a clucking fool not to go to the dance with this hot chick."

Lincoln bolted and waved his chocolate bunny in the air. "I want nothing to do with this!" he yelled over his naked shoulder.

I hoped Josh, Bree's older brother, would feel the same. "I gotta go," I said, hating that I was following Lincoln's lead.

"Don't you want to be here when Josh sees this?" Bree asked as she helped Candace drop nuggets into the bathtub.

"Not really." I headed out, taking care not to step on the nuggets. I pictured how the rest of the evening would go. Mrs. Henderson's lips would be tight with anger over the greasy spots left on the carpet. The dogs would scarf up as many nuggets as they could before any of the Hendersons would realize that the overload of chicken would make them sick. The dogs would barf and then there would be

more than oily stains on the carpet. And Josh...he'd have a date to the dance.

I didn't want to be there when any of that happened.

Melissa Blankly cornered me the next day in the cafeteria. "I know what you're doing," she said, poking me in the chest with her red bejeweled fingernail.

"What are you talking about?" I swatted her hand away and all her bracelets tinkled in response.

She gave me her best mean-girl smile. "You're just reporting on the dance so you can get in."

"Uh, no."

She narrowed her eyes, making her fake lashes look like centipede legs. She opened her mouth to utter another bit of stupidity but closed it fast.

I looked over my shoulder to see why.

Robbie Fisher, the editor-in-chief of the Hartly Herald, strode our way. He placed a large, heavy hand on my shoulder. "Hey, I read the article you submitted to Cox. Good stuff!"

"Thanks!" I responded, flushing from both his praise and closeness.

Robbie was one of the few guys who could wear the Hartly uniform without looking like a dweeb. In fact, with his towering height and broad shoulders, he looked better than most of the males at Hartly, faculty included. "I can't wait to read the rest of it," he said.

"Well, I can't actually finish it until after the dance," I told him.

"Yeah." He nudged me as if we shared a joke. "I got that."

Melissa fluttered her eyelashes at him, but as soon as he left, she ramped up her glare. "Have fun at the dance." It sounded like a threat, but what could she do?

The Hendersons' van pulled up in front of my house the next morning, and Josh tooted the horn. I snagged a muffin off the kitchen table, called goodbye to Uncle Mitch and waved at Mrs. Mateo, our housekeeper, on my way out. After settling in the back seat of the van beside Bree, I gave Josh sitting behind the steering wheel a glance under my lashes. Football had changed him from the lanky kid he used to be. "Is he going to the dance with the chick?" I whispered to Bree.

Bree nodded. "You really should have stuck around. It was pretty hilarious."

"Shut it, Bree," Josh growled without looking at her as he put the van in gear. His voice had also dropped an octave in the last year or so.

"One of the twins let the dogs in," Bree continued.

"Oh no!"

"Yeah," Lincoln piped in. "And that was before Josh got home."

"And then Penguin started vomiting," said Gabby, Bree's baby sister.

"Oh no!" I repeated as if I was surprised. Which I wasn't.

"So basically, Josh followed dog vomit up the stairs," Bree said.

"Mom was so mad!" Lincoln said.

"Shut it, Lincoln," Josh growled as he shifted the van into second gear.

"Josh has to pay for the carpet cleaner," Bree told her.

"Oh, that's not really fair," I said. "I mean, it wasn't his idea—"

"We had to all clean our rooms before the Magic Carpet people came," Gabby said.

"And there isn't even a real magic carpet," one of the twins said.

"Yeah," the identical brother chirped. "It's dumb because it's just a name. They don't fly or anything."

"They don't even pick up stuff--we had to do that," Gabby huffed.

"So, we all pretty much hate that chick," Lincoln said.

I caught Josh's eye in the rearview mirror. His cheeks flooded with color before he fixed his attention on the road.

Later, in my history class, while Mr. Benson talked about the bubonic plague, I thought about how I would ask someone to a dance. I wouldn't spread chicken nuggets around, and I definitely wouldn't call myself a hot chick. I also wouldn't wear a chicken costume. I almost felt sorry for Josh because how could he say no to someone who had spent hundreds of dollars on chicken nuggets/dog treats?

The bell rang before I could come up with my own clever, inexpensive, and not barfing-bad way to ask a guy to a dance.

Troy stood beside my desk and blinked at me through his glasses. The lenses were so thick, they distorted his eyes, giving him a Yoda appearance.

"I'd be honored to go to the dance with you," he said.

We had never actually spoken before, and the normalcy of his voice surprised me. Almost as much as his words. "What?" It was my turn to blink at him.

"The dance," he said. "Thanks for asking. I'd be happy to take you."

"But...I didn't ask you to the dance."

He started to stutter. "Y-you wrote me a letter." He fished in his backpack.

"It must have been a different Evelynn," I told him.

"You're the only Evelynn I know," he said.

I thought about pointing out that we really didn't know each other at all, even though we'd been going to the same school since kindergarten...well, since I was in kindergarten and he was in second grade since he was two grades ahead of me.

He slapped a handwritten note on the desk separating us. Sure enough, it had my name on it, and above that was an invitation to the dance.

"I got the same note." Harrison stood beside Troy and his chin sank to his chest, coming just inches above the Justin Bieber pin fastened to the lapel of his navy blue blazer.

"You did?" My voice squeaked. I cleared it and tried to sound normal.

"I knew it was too good to be true," Harrison said as he scrounged through his leather book bag. Moments later, he pulled out an identical note.

"You could go with both of us," Troy said hopefully.

Harrison looked up and met Troy's gaze. They seemed to come to a silent agreement. "I'd be okay with that."

"But...I'm sorry. I didn't write those. I can't go with a date to the dance. I'm going as a reporter for the Herald."

"I thought only upperclassmen could be on the paper," Troy said.

"Sometimes Cox lets sophomores write guest pieces so he can know who can make the paper as juniors," Harrison told him.

"If you go with us, you don't have to write the article," Troy said.

Harrison straightened his shoulders. "Yeah. We're both upperclassmen, so we're your ticket in."

Troy gave him a high-five.

"But I want to write the article. I want a ticket onto the paper, not to a dance."

The guys both seemed to deflate.

"You can find someone else to go with." I gathered up my books and headed for the science building.

"Yeah? Like who?" Troy demanded, trailing after me.

"I don't know. Who do you want to go with?"

"You," Troy said.

I blew out a breath. "I'm not going to the dance with you! Either of you! I'm sorry!"

"You don't sound sorry," Harrison said before shuffling away in the opposite direction.

"I think you're going to change your mind," Troy said, matching my stride. "When we get to the dance, you're going to feel awkward and alone—being the only sophomore there and all. You'll be glad for my company."

"You better go to class." The bell rang before I could add something mean. I knew the guys weren't to blame. This situation reeked of Melissa.

Troy gave me a determined smile before trotting down the hall.

In biology, I took my usual seat near the window. Most of the class were already in their chairs, but Mr. Beck hadn't arrived yet. Just then the four Lounge Lizards, the barbershop quartet who frequently serenaded students in the cafeteria, positioned themselves in the front of the room directly across from Chester the rat's cage.

"Dance with me when the sun is high," the Lounge Lizards broke out in four-part harmony. "Dance with me beneath the stars."

"Yes, you, Evelynn Marston!" Frankel, a squatty tenor, pointed a finger at me and winked.

Sniggers and laughter broke out around the room.

I bounced to my feet. "What are you talking, huh, singing about?"

Frankel jumped onto a table and wailed, "Let me be with you when the moon is bl-u-e."

Laughter surrounded me and thundered in my ears. Chester the rat squeaked and scampered in his cage. The flames warming the Bunsen burners turned blue and crackled. The electricity in the air fizzled and I felt it lifting my hair off the back of my neck. Heat crawled up my spine and flushed my cheeks. I held out my hands to beg Frankel to stop. The Bunsen burners flashed. The air sparked.

Just then, I was seven years old again and my parents were yelling. My father called my mother a whore. My mother called my father a controlling oaf. The mirror in the hallway shattered. Shards flew around the room like dancing bits of stars caught in a wind tunnel. Stunned, my parents hushed.

"And now we're throwing things. Very mature, Sophia," my dad said.

"I didn't throw anything," my mom said.

Both my parents looked at me.

Screaming shook me out of the memory. Students trampled to exit the room now shimmering in silver smoke. Flames crept up the walls. Colors flashed around me, and I fell to my knees.

Someone grabbed me and lifted me up. I couldn't see her face, but she was small, wiry, and reminded me of my mother. "Mom?"

"She's delirious," a deep voice said.

"Crazy," said a girl's voice—Melissa's. "She'll do anything for a newspaper story."

My knees buckled as I stumbled outside. All around me, kids stood huddled in groups—girls holding each other, boys trying to hide their shock. Teachers yelled at everyone to stay back as the fire consumed what had once been the science building.

A small cheer went up as a kid ducked out of the building holding Chester the rat's cage over his head. Sirens sounded in the distance.

I braced myself against a tree and watched the chaos around me. This is what it's like to witness an ending, I thought. Just like the broken mirror had marked the end of my parents' marriage, I knew that with the destruction of the science building, somehow my life at Hartly would never be the same. It wouldn't be just a matter of new microscopes, desks, tables, chairs, periodic tables, Petri dishes—although all those things would have to be replaced.

Everything would be different now because people would treat me differently, even though I would still be, basically, the same person.

Or so I thought.

Witch One is the prequel to the award-winning novel, Witch Ways.

Indie Artist Press / Brackettville, Texas